A CODE OF CONDUCT

THE MERCENARIES' TALE

CARISSA HARDCASTLE

HARDCASTLE PUBLISHING HOUSE

A *Code of Conduct* is a fantasy story with dark themes and depictions of violence, murder, strong language, sex, and drug and alcohol use.

Additionally, this story contains torture, blood play, attempted sexual assault, and mentions of child abuse.

A quick note

A *Code of Conduct* takes place during the same timeline as *Mountains Will Crumble*, and is meant to be read after or in tandem, but **not** before.

If you'd like to read them in tandem, here is a guide for the best experience:

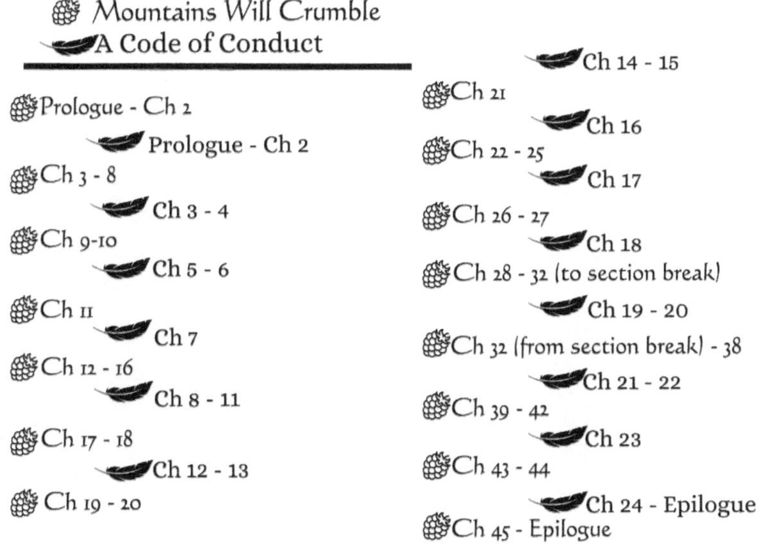

Characters

<u>The Mercenaries</u>

Jasper (jAs-per)	33	fair folk (fae)	14yrs a merc
Aleah (uh-lee-uh)	23	half fae/human	9yrs a merc
Leonidas (lee-oh-nI-dihs)	29	human	8yrs a merc
Campbell (kAm-behl)	25	fair folk (fae)	4yrs a merc
Calysta (kuh-lihs-tuh)	169	fair folk (nymph)	4yrs a merc

<u>The Royal Guard</u>

Merriam (mair-ee-uhm)	25	Marshal of Sekha	human
Pos Ferrick (pahs Fair-ihck)	321	Captain of the Guard	high fae
Kottor Dio (kaht-or Dee-oh)	244	Ranger | Commander	high fae
Eskar (ehsk-ar)	128	Ranger | Commander	high fae
Rovin Arwood (rah-vihn Ar-wUd)	28	Ranger | Lieutenant	half-fae/human
Kodi (koh-dee)	26	Ranger	high fae
Bellamy (behl-uh-mee)	20	Ranger	high fae

<u>**The Stonebane Line**</u>

Regenya 414 Keeper
  (reh-jehn-yuh)
Darius   371 high fae
  (dair-ee-us)
Mollian   25 Keeper
  (mahl-ee-ehn)
Ryddan   6 Keeper/half-demon
  (rihd-ehn)

<u>**Overseers & Others**</u>

Spiro Kinbriar   247 Overseer of Do Lech   high fae
  (spee-roh Kihn-brI-ar)
Larna Kinbriar   153 Overseer of Do Lech   high fae
  (lar-nuh Kihn-brI-ar)
Chetney Kinbriar 42 heir to Do Lech   high fae
  (cheht-nee Kihn-brI-ar)
Illiziana Fielder   239 Overseer of Red Marsh high fae
  (ihl-ihzee-ah-nuh feel-der)
Shiloh   24 street performer   fair folk (fae)
  (shI-loh)
Lydia   109 nursemaid   high fae
  (lih-dee-uh)
Novi   174 wood nymph   fair folk (nymph)
  (noh-vee)
Horscha   130 aviculturist   high fae
  (hor-shuh)

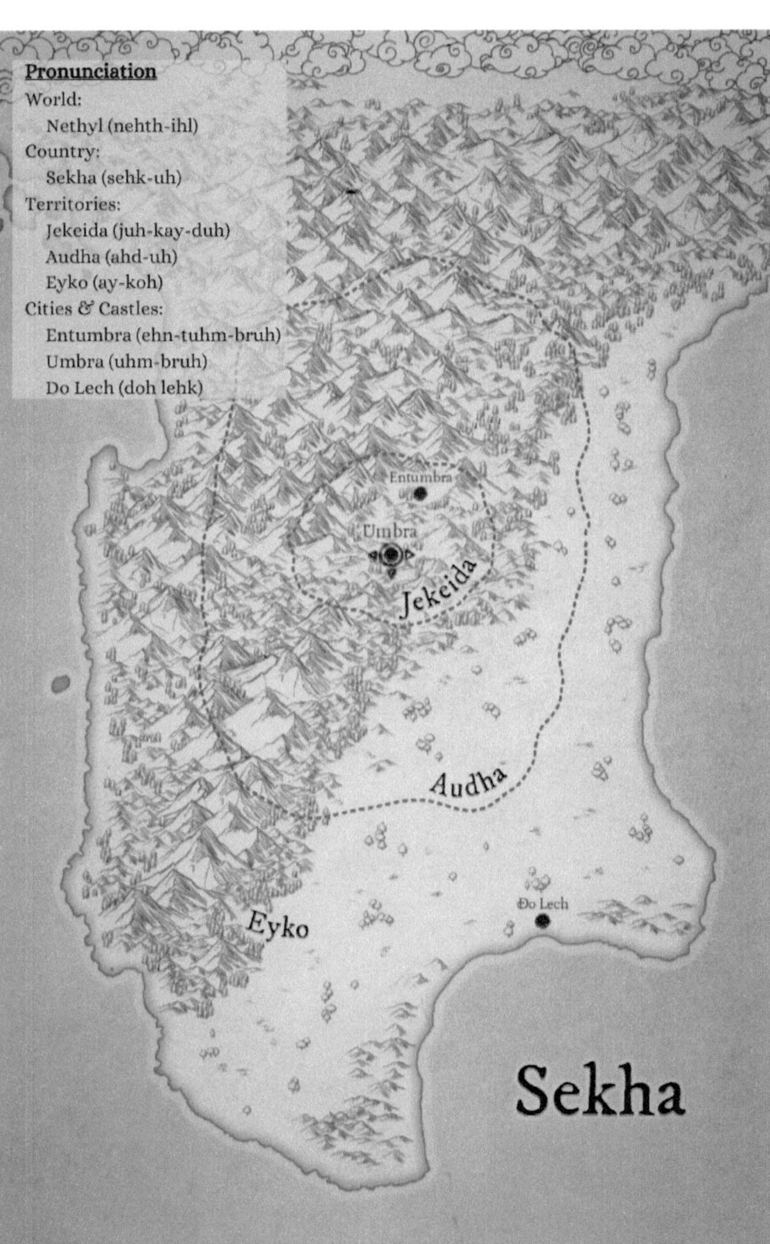

Pronunciation
World:
Nethyl (nehth-ihl)
Country:
Sekha (sehk-uh)
Territories:
Jekeida (juh-kay-duh)
Audha (ahd-uh)
Eyko (ay-koh)
Cities & Castles:
Entumbra (ehn-tuhm-bruh)
Umbra (uhm-bruh)
Do Lech (doh lehk)
Entumbra
Umbra
Jekeida
Audha
Do Lech
Eyko
Sekha

To Josh, whose morals are white as a dove, but still loves just as fiercely
as any blood-spilling hero.

Prologue

The trees know

110 years before …

CALYSTA LAY IN A field, eyes closed against the sun's brightness and hands twirling and folding through the air as she manipulated the plants around her. Blades of grass grew up and over her legs, whispering against olive green skin as they wrapped around her. Bright yellow daisies threaded through the lengths of her hair, contrasting with the soft pink strands.

"Calysta!" The call echoed across the meadow, and Calysta stilled her hands at her sides. "Calyyyystaaa!"

With a sigh, she dropped her hold on the plants, letting them recede to their natural state as she rolled over and raised herself onto an elbow. "Over here."

Novi, another wood nymph, ran over, dropping to their knees in the grass. "What are you doing out here? The festival is starting soon!"

Calysta dug the claws of one hand into the dirt, breathing in the scent of clean, damp earth when she pulled free. "It's so quiet here, and so open. I was just … taking a moment to breathe it in."

Novi clicked their tongue against pointed teeth. "You're around the high fae too much."

Calysta smiled, letting Novi pull her up when they stood. "The cities fascinate me. Can you imagine feeling the need to create a space so permanent? To dedicate your whole, long life to one area?"

Novi rolled their eyes, still holding Calysta's hand. "Absolutely not."

Nymphs, while not technically nomadic, lived very flexible and mostly solitary lives. Their major concern always lay with tending the nature of their magic. Wood nymphs kept to the forests and grasslands, water nymphs to the lakes, seas, and rivers. Between the two, most of the world was covered, watched over.

And then there were the wild nymphs, who belonged to neither the trees nor the waves, but had a deeper connection to the sentient creatures of the world. They were few and far between, and had once been hunted and presumed dangerous for their perceived control over living things.

It wasn't control, though, not really. A wood nymph could call forth a bramble and ask it to grow, but the bramble would eventually do the same if left alone; the nymph's magic only helped it along the way. A wild nymph's magic could only grow and guide the wants of a creature, though the high fae never took the time to figure that out. Nor did the humans, who, as a species, were threatened by magic they'd never been blessed with.

From the time they were old enough to be self-sufficient, most nymphs struck out on their own, finding a patch of forest or sea to call home until they felt the tug to move elsewhere. Nymphs were connected to Nethyl more than they ever were to each other. Familial bonds were nothing more than occasional company and the knowledge that they weren't truly alone.

But there were occasions when they would gather. Once every ten years, nymphs would group together on the night when both of Nethyl's moons were full, celebrating the world they called home and pooling their magic to sink back into the earth, giving the planet new life and renewed energy.

Calysta had attended only three others, though she was now fifty-nine. At twenty-nine and thirty-nine she'd been too busy exploring the depths of her own magic and learning more about the plants she could manipulate to join in the festivities.

Calysta glanced up into the aspens as Novi pulled her along, running through the forest at a gleeful pace. The leaves high above trembled as a gust of wind blew through them, whispering soft words of contentment to each other.

Novi ignored them, but Calysta looked up, letting tendrils of her magic caress the branches, the trees swaying to watch her as she ran.

She slammed into Novi's back, getting a mouthful of deep indigo hair. She spluttered, pushing Novi's hair away, but they reached around and pressed their palm to her lips.

Calysta stilled, standing on her toes to peer over Novi's shoulder as they dropped their hand.

"It's not right, Spiro. I can feel the disturbance it causes. Do Lech was built right over a ley line that connects directly to Entumbra. Allowing the nymphs to hold their festival outside of your city is dangerous!"

"These festivals have been happening much longer than either of us have been alive, Illiziana." Spiro scratched his cheek through the fire-red hair of his beard. "The Stonebanes have no qualms with them. Don't you think that if this were something that could harm the Gate, the Keepers would have outlawed it long ago?"

Illiziana's hands clenched into fists. "I'm sure the Stonebanes are pre-occupied with running a country and monitoring the Gate. They might not care about the nymph population enough to monitor it. Besides, there are so few of them. The princess hasn't even taken up her post in Entumbra yet, and I'm sure Their Majesties are soaking up whatever time they have left with their daughter still in Umbra."

Spiro sighed, pinching the bridge of his nose. "Is there a point to this, Illiziana?"

Illiziana bristled, bright blue eyes shining with anger. "We need to maintain control, Spiro. Do Lech may have been given to you by birthright, but I have won Red Marsh through years of hard work and dedication. Do you not realize that our cities are at the mercy of both wood and water nymphs? We're sandwiched between the forests and the sea, with nothing but small settlements between us and Jekeida."

Spiro narrowed his eyes at the dark-skinned fae beside him. "You dare to question my right to rule Do Lech or my dedication to seeing my city thrive?"

Illiziana dragged her hands down her face, a rueful laugh bubbling from her chest. She reached out, grabbing Spiro by the shoulders. "Why do we keep ending up at each other's throats? We're both overseers; we both care about our cities and understand that South Eyko is far from the eyes of the Umbra. We govern ourselves."

Spiro nodded.

"I didn't mean to sound accusatory, and I didn't mean to get defensive. I just want your help, Spiro. Your family is the most influential in the country, second only to the Stonebanes. I'm telling you, as an equal, as a *friend*, that I can feel these rituals affect Nethyl. There's already a heavy concentration of magical activity in Do Lech, adding to that with the undiluted power of the nymphs ... it's dangerous."

Spiro sighed. "What do you need from me?"

"Watch their ritual tonight. If you think I'm being hysterical, fine. But if you feel uneasy, if you can feel the way the magic alters the fabric of our universe ... help me set up legislation. Help me put boundaries in place to protect us and our people."

"Okay, I'll keep an open mind," Spiro agreed, and relief flooded Illiziana's face.

As the two fae walked away, Novi shoved Calysta backwards, holding up their hand to create a wall of brush to hide their retreat. Novi's black eyes gleamed dangerously. "The fae are getting ballsy."

Calysta licked her lips, uneasy. "*We're* fae, Novi."

Novi scoffed. "Not like them."

Acid turned in Calysta's stomach at Novi's tone, and she fought off a shiver, crossing her arms over her belly and tipping her head back to look at the trees. All her life, she'd heard that the high fae thought themselves superior, even though it was the nymphs that held a blood connection to the world. The nymphs were still fae, though, and Calysta had seen a level of camaraderie amongst both high fae and other classes of fair folk that nymphs never had.

She was jealous of that companionship, though she would never voice that feeling. Nymphs belonged to the world, to nature, but she sometimes thought it might be nice to belong to a family, to people who made her wants and well-being a priority.

"Not like them," she whispered, feeling an ache in her chest.

Novi nodded, unaware of Calysta's inner turmoil. "They hate us for our magic. They envy what we have and what we do for Nethyl. Of course they're going to try to limit us."

Calysta made a non-committal noise in response, reaching down to clasp Novi's hand. "Let's just hurry up and meet with the others. Everything will be fine. Besides, the only fae who rule the nymphs are the Stonebanes, and they know where they got their power. Don't stress over it, okay? Tonight is a celebration. Let's have fun!"

By the time the moons rose in the sky, Calysta was drunk, her earlier unease completely forgotten. She'd lost count of how many glasses of the tart, berry wine she'd had, knowing only that she was here with her people, and she was happy.

The grass was soft and warm under her bare feet, and she twirled in a circle, holding the hands of the nymphs on either side of her as they sang a melody to the plants and the water and magic of Nethyl. Novi's eyes met hers from across the circle, a mischievous gleam in them. Calysta loosened her grip on the hands she held just as Novi dropped, causing the nymphs on either side to tumble to the ground and creating a chain reaction.

Calysta also fell to the grass, catching herself as laughter pulled from her chest. A few of the older nymphs were walking around, handing out stalky, gray-skinned mushrooms. Calysta took the few that were offered to her, holding them in her hand as she caught her breath. Novi wandered over, raising their handful in a toast before tipping the contents back into their mouth.

Calysta copied the gesture. The mushrooms were a stiff but airy texture, collapsing easily between her sharp teeth. Their flavor was musky, but didn't linger long after Calysta swallowed them down.

She folded her legs in front of her, once again letting her magic loose to manipulate the grass around her. She wove her fingers through the blades that grew and flowered at her bequest. Her body started to feel heavy, her muscles relaxing and letting her sink deeper into the ground below her. As she continued to play with the grass, she looked up to the aspens lining one side of the meadow, watching the wind move through them, pulling the leaves this way and that until the golden hearts drifted to the forest floor.

Euphoric laughter spilled from her lips, and her gaze wandered the clearing, searching for … Calysta frowned, sitting up straighter. She'd been looking for someone, someone she was connected to, but the daunting feeling that she was alone here threatened to overwhelm her.

She shook off the emotion, pushing to stand and wander over to the stream that cut through the meadow. As soon as she stood, Calysta felt impossibly light, and a smile stretched across her face. She crouched at the edge of the water, dipping a hand into it and marveling at the way it rushed through her fingers.

The water crawled up her arm, swirling just below her elbow, and she fell onto her bottom with a gasp as the water dropped back into the stream. She looked up to see a blue-skinned water nymph laughing at her, not at all malicious, just enjoying letting his magic play. "I didn't mean to startle you," he assured her.

Calysta shook her head, reaching out a hand again to let him curl the water around her skin. "It's beautiful," she told him, watching the moonlight glimmer in the water. Her own magic pulsed inside her, and with a single relaxing breath, she'd freed it, letting it wander over the grass and wildflowers that lined the streambank. She could feel the plants moving and growing, not so much responding to her as using her to do what they would.

She laughed again, watching a vine curl through the water before lifting her gaze to the trees. *They know,* she thought. *The trees know.*

Novi found their way to her side, settling down on the bank and dipping their toes in the water. Magic flowed from the three of them, leaves and water winding together.

Before long, each of the nymphs in the clearing had gathered along the stream, and as the late autumn moons hung in the sky, the nymphs started a song, more melody than any real words. Calysta felt the hum in her chest before she realized she was singing along, her magic winding with those around her until she almost couldn't tell what was hers and what was others'.

Her head swam, the colors of the world vivid and seeming to sparkle before her eyes. She drew one claw down her forearm, forcing it into her skin until bright, shimmery blood flowed down her arm and into the grass below her. She pressed her palms against the ground, feeling the warmth of her blood freed from her body, just as her magic had been.

Tilting her head back to stare at the stars, she continued singing with the others, pressing her palms against the earth and channeling her magic down, down, down.

Calysta's breaths came faster when she felt something deep below Nethyl's surface. A river of magic flowed beneath where the nymphs were gathered, and when her own power touched it, she felt the magic that composed the world latch onto it, pulling it along so quickly that it stole the breath from Calysta's lungs.

She realized that the other nymphs had gone quiet, each of them also feeding their magic to the vein below them, and a surge of fear pulled from her gut. She started to pull her hand away, but Novi's fingers brushed against hers, and she turned her eyes to meet theirs.

"We give to Nethyl as Nethyl gives to us." Novi smiled, gesturing with their chin toward the treeline in the distance. "The trees know, Calysta."

Calysta glanced at the aspens, their leaves all golds and reds. Her magic still poured from her into the ground, but she didn't feel weak. No, as she watched the trees respond to the wind, one after the other as it blew through them before sweeping across the meadow to lift the hair from her shoulders, she felt powerful. She felt ... seen.

Chapter 1

New rule

"LONG, LONG AGO, WHEN classism ruled Sekha, there lived a powerful fae who fell in love with a human. The fae was a commander in the Royal Guard, and even rumored to be the next captain."

"He wasn't a Ranger; he couldn't have been Captain of the Guard."

A log in the fire cracked, shooting embers into the air. Flames danced in the wind, casting flickering shadows across the clearing.

"Shhh." Aleah glared at the male across from her. "He was rumored to be the next captain," she reiterated, gaze moving back to the fire and unfocusing as she talked. Her fingers absently drifted through the short, soft curls of the Ranger whose head rested in her lap. "He and the human married, but had to keep it a secret due to the aforementioned classism. Even with the secrecy, he was still able to secure his wife a position in the castle as handmaid to the queen, because of his status."

"No, she was already the queen's handmaid. That's how they met in the first place."

Aleah's fingers stilled, hazel eyes rolling to the sky. "New rule, take a drink every time Campbell interrupts."

"I'm just trying to keep the historical accuracy." Campbell touched a hand to his chest defensively, but still brought his cup up with the other and took a long swig of mead.

"It's a Legend, dickweed. It's famously *not* historically accurate." Aleah scowled, irritably brushing strands of bright red hair back behind her ear, the pointed tip clipped flat.

Kodi raised a cup into her line of vision, amusement dancing in his bi-colored eyes as she took it without glancing down.

"Where do you think Legends come from, smart one? They're all based in history," Campbell argued. A dead leaf floated down on the breeze, catching in a fork of his antlers.

"Do you need me to define 'based' for you?" Aleah retorted before turning a pleading look at Leonidas, who sat next to Campbell.

The human raised an arm to pluck the leaf free, firelight playing across the colorful tattoos of various birds that covered his skin. "Nope, I'm not involved."

While Aleah and Campbell continued bickering, Panic surveyed the clearing on the outskirts of Umbra in which they sat. He was perched in the boughs of a pine, close enough to see and hear everything, but far enough away from the fire's light as to stay hidden in the shadows.

A field mouse crept cautiously toward the edge of the clearing, little nose twitching as it smelled the food the people had brought with them.

Panic took half a second to look back at Leonidas. The man hadn't given him any specific commands and was clearly occupied with the others, and that was enough for the peregrine falcon.

He dove from the tree, stretching out his feet and flaring his wings just before he hit the ground. Scooping the mouse up in his talons, Panic squeezed, snapping its neck before it even had a chance to squeak, and flew back up to perch in the tree.

"As I was saying, the human girl was a handmaid to the queen, and the two became very close friends."

A wet rip cut through the air as Panic tore the head from the field mouse, tipping his head back to swallow. Aleah's eyes flicked up to him for a brief moment, but she didn't falter in her story.

"Before long, both the human and the queen she served fell pregnant. It was an arduous time for them, but they had each other to lean on, as well as their husbands. During the course of her pregnancy, the human told the queen of her husband's status as a commander and shared her worries of the discrimination their child would encounter. Humans were considered lower-class citizens because of their inability to wield magic and lack of inherent protection from it, but to be half-human was even worse. What an abomination, to desecrate a fae's pure blood." Aleah's voice remained clear as she talked, but Kodi squeezed her thigh just the same.

Panic had made quick work of his mouse and was now settled contently on the branch, feathers puffed against the slight chill of the late summer air as he listened to the tale. He couldn't understand any of the words, of course, but he understood the cadence of the voices below him. Their effortless camaraderie always put him at ease, and he would go into much the same sort of trance as anyone when a story was being told, content to be here with his people and absorbing their happiness.

"The queen vowed to keep the child's halfling heritage a secret and to ensure that they always had a place in her court. Before long, both babies were born. The queen's was a girl, second born and heir to the throne of Sekha, and her handmaid's child a boy. Sadly, the human died shortly after childbirth—"

"No, she didn't. She stayed working for the queen, but never claimed the child as her own to hide his parentage," Campbell interjected.

Leonidas and Kodi raised their drinks, the Ranger spilling a good bit down the front of his shirt from his prone position.

Aleah swallowed the rest of her mead, wiping a hand over her mouth as she continued without commenting on the antlered male's interjection. "And the half-fae and the princess were raised together. They were best friends and decided when they were merely five years old that there would never be anyone else for either of them. The whims of children are often fleeting, but their bond held true, their love for one another growing and maturing as they did. They married in secret at twenty-four, right before the princess went off to Entumbra to study at the Gate for five long years."

Panic's head dipped as Aleah's voice lulled him into a light sleep. He would be awake and alert with a mere snap of Leonidas' fingers, but for now he let himself drift, feeling the wind in his feathers and the slight pull of the planet's magnetic poles as birds did with the changing seasons. *Follow the warmth*, a part of his mind whispered, but a stronger, much louder part of him knew that he would never leave the human. He loved Leonidas. Campbell and Merriam, too, but to a much lesser degree.

Panic stirred slightly at the thought of the blonde girl. He looked around the clearing, but already knew she wasn't there. It felt like ages since she'd come back to coo pretty things at him and feed him scraps of meat. Though she'd never lived full time at the merc house, she'd been an almost constant presence for years, until suddenly she just wasn't.

Merriam still came by, of course, but less frequently due to her appointment as marshal, and Panic was disgruntled to realize that he missed her.

"They kept their marriage a secret for years and years and years. They never even Bonded, because they didn't trust a fae tattooer to keep their secret for them, and the humans of Earth were still much spread out and distrusting of strangers. After two hundred years together, they both longed for a child. As we know, marriage has never mattered in Sekha's monarchs. As long as the ruling Keeper produces an heir to take charge of the Gate and an heir to take the throne, Sekha and Nethyl remain safe. So, still hiding the secret of their marriage, our star-crossed lovers decided to accept whatever may come of a Keeper born from one half-fae parent," Aleah continued, unaware of Panic's brooding in the tree above.

"The now-queen eventually gave birth to a prince. He had her dark skin, white hair, and green eyes, but only time would tell if he possessed her magic. His name was Dain, and this is his Legend."

"Storytelling works better if you say what it's about in the beginning," Campbell couldn't help mumbling the interjection, already bringing his drink to his lips.

Aleah stole a sip from Kodi. "As the firstborn, Dain's destiny was to guard the Gate beneath Entumbra and know its magic inside and out. His magic manifested early on, and he was Casting to his mother before he could even speak full sentences. Dain was a natural when it came to communicating with the Gate, easily able to understand what it needed from him, and he was eager to begin his life in Entumbra. He was the first Keeper in history ever to be born from a parent who wasn't high fae. Because of how strongly Dain's magic manifested, his parents made knowledge of their marriage public. Though there was a bit of unrest regarding a half-fae king, Dain was clearly, undoubtedly, a Keeper, which helped keep most of the country happy. After his younger brother was born about a hundred years later—"

It was actually one hundred and sixty years, Campbell thought, finishing off his mead and resting his head against Leonidas' shoulder. The blonde leaned into him, his own head putting pressure against

Campbell's antlers in a comfortably familiar way. Campbell snaked his arm around Leonidas' and threaded their fingers together as happiness ran through him along with the alcohol. "I love you," he whispered. Firelight danced in his indigo eyes before they slipped closed.

"Are you drunk, buck?" Leonidas asked quietly, a chuckle rumbling through him.

"Mmm," Campbell replied.

Leonidas turned his head, nose brushing through Campbell's dark curls as he pressed his lips to the male's temple. "I love you."

"—they knew that Keeper blood always ran true. It doesn't matter who the parents are, as long as one of them has Keeper blood, that is the only blood that will be passed on to the child," Aleah prattled on.

Panic's head snapped up. He stood straight, listening to the forest around him. Aleah's voice. The crackle of the fire. The whispered conversation of the males below him. A small creature snuffled around in the foliage underneath his tree.

The falcon stretched out his wings, taking off into the night. Leonidas glanced up at the sound of his departure, but soon turned his attention back to his friends and the fire. Aleah was close to finishing her telling of the Legend, and Campbell perked back up, ready to take over the role of storyteller.

Panic cleared the treetops, soaring above the mountains as his eyes scanned the forest below. He was fast, leaving Umbra behind within minutes. Eventually, he lighted on a scraggly branch toward the top of a mountain, staring south. He ruffled his feathers, cocking his head to the side as he blinked. *Follow the warmth.* That thing inside him once again tugged, but it was a quiet instinct that he'd been ignoring for years and never once obeyed, so quiet now it barely even registered.

It wasn't migration that pulled him south, but something else. Being a falcon, he'd never thought to question how he navigated the skies or what pulled him. But his time among people had heightened his perception of the world around him. He was more alert to changes in the atmosphere and the presence of others, which had saved Leonidas' skin on more than one occasion.

Panic flared his wings and screeched. He'd felt a disturbance from the south, something shifting, and it made him uneasy.

He scanned the dark horizon for a few more seconds, watching with a glare that was pure predator. Then he leapt from his perch and into the wind, rising high into the sky to circle back toward Leonidas and the others.

Chapter 2

I'm not drama

ALEAH SAT AT THE end of the bar with a cup of fruit tea, the caffeine wholly necessary after her inadvertently late night telling stories around the fire. Though her posture was casual, the unconcealed dagger strapped to her thigh was not.

Sunlight spilled through the threshold as the door was opened, nervous tension rolling from the figure that stepped through. The water nymph lowered the hood from his face as he looked around the bar. His skin was dark blue, and his long, slate-gray hair was tied back from his face. Inky black eyes lit with surprise as they landed on Aleah.

The nymph flicked his gaze to the bartender, the question clear on his face.

The bartender gave a single nod, lifting his shoulders in a shrug as he continued drying the glass in his hand.

Aleah grinned with her teeth when the nymph's eyes turned back to her, and his brow furrowed as he walked over, hands twisting into the folds of his cloak. "You're Aleah?" His musical voice was soft and quiet.

She raised her cup in affirmation. "How might I assist, good sir?"

He slid onto a barstool next to her, unable to hide his discomfort. "You're young."

Aleah rolled her eyes and chugged the rest of her tea. "You're blue." She wiped the back of her hand across her mouth.

The nymph swallowed, looking around the mostly empty tavern. "How does this work? Do I order a drink?"

"Do you want a drink?" Aleah raised a brow, hazel eyes glittering with amusement in the dim light.

The nymph wet his lips before clearing his throat. "I've never ..." he trailed off.

Pushing her cup to the side, Aleah propped her elbow on the bar and rested her chin in her palm to watch him. "Never hired someone to go around the law for you?"

"Ineedsomeonedead," he finally said, running the words together in his haste to get them out.

Aleah's eyes widened, a dangerous smile stretching her lips. "Who?"

"A fae named Illiziana Fielder. And it needs to be discreet. She's an overseer in South Eyko."

The mention of the southern territory sent a cold tremor running through the mercenary. She swallowed against the old remnants of fear that crawled up her throat as her mouth went dry. The scars that decorated her torso seemed to burn where the fabric of her shirt brushed against them, and her vision started to tunnel.

One hand dropped nonchalantly to her lap, and she curled her fingers into her thigh in an attempt to ground herself with the discomfort. "What town?" She forced her breathing to remain even. South Eyko was a wide expanse of land; it would take several weeks to traverse the entire area. What were the odds that this job would take Aleah back to her roots?

"Red Marsh, a small fishing port close to Do Lech."

If it weren't for the pulse pounding in her ears, Aleah would have thought her heart had stopped beating as her entire body went cold. Of course it was by Do Lech.

"We are prepared to pay very handsomely, considering her station," the nymph continued, oblivious to Aleah's inner turmoil.

Tell him no, a small voice in her head pleaded. *We don't have to go, we can't go.* With great effort, she peeled her tongue from where it seemed fixed to the roof of her mouth. "That's at least a week's worth of travel just for the journey down there. I'll need compensation for lodging and supplies on the road." That hadn't been what she'd expected to tell him, and she couldn't hold back a blink of surprise after the words left her.

He nodded, "Of course, of course. That won't be a problem at all."

"Good." Aleah smiled, reaching for her cup before remembering it was empty. She ran her hands over her thighs, her palms clammy, and cleared her throat. *Okay, we're doing this, then. Not a problem. Not for us, no sir! Legends, merc, you're fucking losing it.* With a sharp shake of her head, she pushed back the encroaching mania that wound its way through her and rested her hands on the bartop. "I'll work up a cost analysis tonight and have it sent to wherever you're staying while here. This kind of job will require payment in full upfront, I'm sure you understand. Clients don't typically like to give too much personal information with this type of request, which makes them hard to track down, and I can't have you squirreling out on me."

Now it was the nymph's turn to blink in surprise, his black eyes growing wide. "Do you not wish to know my justification for the request?"

Aleah rolled her eyes, digging in her pocket for some coppers to leave on the bar. "You said she works in politics?"

"Yes."

"Then I guarantee you she's done some crooked shit. Where should I send the contract?" In her line of work, contracts were more a request for payment than anything, but the formality of them often made clients feel more secure.

"The inn off East Street, do you know it?"

"Yes, I'm familiar. Be waiting in the lobby about an hour after nightfall. I'll have the papers delivered there."

The nymph faltered, wringing his hands together. "How are we to know you will hold up your end of the deal?"

Aleah gave him an unamused look, lips pressed flat together. "I've got a reputation to uphold. That's how you found me, right?" She slid from her stool, not waiting for him to argue or reply.

Bright sunlight blinded her as she left the tavern, and she pulled the hood of her cowl up over her face to shield it. Her fingers flexed at her sides as she walked, focused on keeping deep, even breaths.

Do Lech. She was going to Do Lech.

Admitting it to herself caused her stomach to lurch aggressively, and she sidestepped into an alley to spill her guts.

"Well, that's an entirely unfortunate reaction," she grumbled, wiping the back of a shaking hand across her lips.

It's been years, she thought. *We've grown past this. And we're not going to Do Lech, just nearby. Nobody will know we're there. Nobody even remembers us.*

She waited a few moments, making sure the urge to vomit had fully passed before leaving the alley. The walk back to the mercenary house was completed solely on muscle memory, Aleah's mind blank rather than dealing with the prospect of facing her past. She walked through the back door, closing it behind her and leaning against it as she let out a soft breath.

The world started to come back into focus with the familiarity of her home. *We're worrying over nothing,* she mentally reiterated before that tiny voice could re-conjure those fears.

She moved through the main room—which she'd dubbed the mushroom years ago in joking allusion to the fact that it had no windows—directly into the kitchen, tipping her face under the tap to rinse her mouth. Once her mouth felt clean, she rummaged around in the cabinets in search of a sweet snack to settle what was left of her nerves.

The door on the opposite side of the mushroom opened, but she didn't turn.

"How did your meeting go?" Jasper asked, walking over to fill a cup from the sink. His black-feathered wings were tucked close to his back to keep from hitting her, his dark skin shining with sweat from whatever circuit he'd run in the training room.

A strangled laugh fell from her lips. "Well, I have a job. And it's very good pay."

Jasper watched her, waiting. In the years since taking her in and training her as a mercenary, he'd learned how to read her stress cues well. He also knew better than anyone how to handle that stress in a way that both worked for her and was good for her.

"Someone wants a politician taken out. Low-level, it won't be a problem," she added, waving a hand dismissively.

Jasper nodded, continuing to watch her as he drank.

"It will require some travel. Well, a lot of travel." Aleah grabbed a loaf of bread, cutting a slice before pulling out a jar of nut butter to spread over it and drizzling it with honey. She took a bite. "It's down south."

Jasper's wings flared slightly, but that was his only outward sign of surprise. "Where down south?"

Aleah took another bite, shrugging even as the first pricks of true panic worked their way out from her center. "A fishing port. Red Marsh?"

"Are you taking the job?"

"Yup," she said to her food, concentrating on shutting off the alarm bells that rang in her head.

Not safe not safe not safe, they called to her.

Shut up shut up shut up, she hissed back.

Silver eyes searched her face. Jasper knew she hadn't been back to South Eyko since she'd left over ten years before. "Aleah."

The redhead met his gaze, continuing to eat. "What?"

"You don't have to do this."

Aleah narrowed her eyes, shoving the last bit of bread into her mouth and taking her time to finish it. She forced her movements to be measured and purposeful, knowing he was expecting her to fall apart. But she wasn't a child anymore. She was beyond whatever insipid little fears her uncle had instilled in her when she was young. When Jasper still hadn't moved or said anything else by the time she swallowed, she brushed off her hands with a pointed sigh. "I'm going to go draw up a contract." She walked past him.

Jasper grabbed her arm. "Stop. Take a moment to breathe."

"I'm not a fucking child, Jasper." Aleah ripped her arm free. "It's a job and I'm taking it and it doesn't matter how close it is to Do Lech because I'm grown now and he doesn't have power over me anymore and he can't—" Aleah's words caught in her throat as the crippling fear and dread she'd lived with for so many years crashed across her in an all-consuming wave. Tears rushed to her eyes, and she couldn't hold them back. "He doesn't have power over me anymore," she insisted, a small sob following the words.

Jasper spread an arm, and Aleah stumbled into his embrace, his wings wrapping around her protectively. She cried fully then, and he let her, standing strong and solid and silent.

When she finally pushed back, she wiped the heels of her hands against her eyes and cleared away the tear tracks on her cheeks. "Fuck. I need to pull it together."

"You were physically and mentally abused for almost a decade, Aleah. Going back is going to play with your stability," Jasper said softly.

Already pulling back against her old fears and shoving them into that dark place she never examined too closely, Aleah grimaced. "Do you ever get tired of taking care of us all the time?"

"Oh, absolutely I do," he deadpanned. "But then I think about how dull it would be going back to being on my own, and I remind myself that all of the drama is worth it."

"I'm not drama," she defended.

Jasper didn't even bother to reply.

"Wanna help me write up an expected expenses report?" she asked.

He laughed. "Not even remotely, but if you'd like, the books could use a once-over."

"You've got it, boss." Aleah saluted before bounding up the steps.

She loved numbers. They made sense, and they never changed. Numbers made up the entire world, too. Everything could be figured out with the right equation, and figuring out answers to those problems settled Aleah's mind in ways not much else could.

Even though it was entirely simple math, calculating budgets and expenses was almost Aleah's favorite part of every job. She knew the books for the mercenary troupe were solid, of course, and that Jasper had just asked her as an extra form of distraction, but she'd look them over when she was done with her new contract regardless.

Aleah rifled through the desk drawers, flipping through different folders until she found an empty expense sheet. She'd drafted up a template a few years back after Jasper and Leonidas went through a phase of forgetting to account for one expense or another on any given job. She smiled fondly, remembering the warmth that had spread through her when Jasper praised her work. It had felt good to contribute something lasting, to have done something that felt simple to her but was so appreciated by the others.

Once the expected costs for travel and board were written up, she calculated her usual fee for her time, added charges for the government involvement and the murder aspect, and wrote it all up into a contract. The wording was simple, referencing only "the job" and missing all specific details. When she was satisfied, she signed it, her agreement that the job would be complete within a month once payment was provided, and slipped out of the room.

She climbed the stairs to the roof, winding her way carefully through the garden Calysta tended there. The nymph also slept under the open sky among her plants most nights. Only inclement weather brought her inside, other than the rare occasions the whole group went on a job together and spent the first night back on the floor of the mushroom.

Once away from the plants, Aleah fell into a sprint and launched herself from the edge, landing nimbly on the neighboring roof. She entered the building through a small door, the cacophony of various birds chirping and ruffling their wings filling the air.

She ignored the many different roosts, perches, and cages as she made her way downstairs to the ground level. "Hey, Horscha," Aleah greeted the fae perched behind the counter next to the front door. She had long, dark hair pulled up into a ponytail and deep gold eyes. She'd been helping Leonidas run his aviary for a few years, but had been caring for homing pigeons for hundreds of years before that.

"If you're looking for Leo, he took some of the hawks out for a hunt early this morning. Won't be expecting him back until this evening at the earliest," Horscha greeted, dropping her feet from where they rested on the counter.

"Actually, I need to have a message sent to the couriers. I require an errand boy." Aleah propped her elbows against the counter with a winning smile.

Horscha raised one well-manicured eyebrow, dropping from her stool to pull out a small strip of paper and a pen and slide it over to the redhead.

Aleah scribbled a quick note. "Put it on my tab," she requested cheerfully.

Horscha tightly rolled the paper, tying it off before selecting a pigeon from a blue cage, the color designated for the birds who called the courier's roost home. "You don't have a tab," she said simply, attaching the note to the jesses on the pigeon's legs.

"Oh, that's right. Tell Leo I owe him one." Aleah blew the fae a kiss before sliding out the front door.

Chapter 3
Barmaid

ALEAH HAD ALWAYS PREFERRED company to solitude, but the days following her acceptance of the job in Red Marsh, companionship became a necessity. She didn't tell herself that her panic and fear were ridiculous because she didn't give herself the chance to acknowledge their existence, much less sit with them. She followed Jasper around town as he met with informants, helped Leonidas gather pigeons and ravens for transport to other parts of Sekha, cooked meals with Campbell when he refused to let her accompany him on his jobs, assisted Calysta when she went to market to sell herbal remedies and tinctures, and spent every other waking moment with Kodi when he wasn't on duty.

Despite her erratic emotions and quickly fraying nerves, Aleah was still a professional and did start to work out the details of travel and other preparations whenever Jasper or Leonidas were in the office. But once she heard that an official group from Umbra would be heading to her former home, she stalled, weighing whether or not it would be best to wait until after that envoy left to avoid bringing attention back north. As far as she knew, everyone who'd known the child she'd been thought she was dead, and she very much wanted to keep it that way. It was easier—less messy—to pretend she'd never been a Kinbriar.

But then Merriam had returned from Entumbra, and Aleah learned that her dearest friend would be part of the group negotiating plans for the new transportation system Mollian had proposed. That probably shouldn't have swayed her as heavily as it did. The reasons for waiting were still valid, but she missed seeing Merriam every day, and the thought of having all of that travel time together was too tempting to pass up.

So when they'd all gone out to drink, and alcohol burned warm and worry-free through her blood, Aleah told Merriam she wanted to go to Do Lech with her before she could overthink it. Of course, everyone else chimed in about how she'd been so off kilter since taking the job, but Kodi had shown up and saved her from having to defend herself or acknowledge they were right.

After what could only be described as a delightful drinking game between her, Merriam, Kodi, and Rovin, Aleah found herself drunk, happy, and perched on Kodi's shoulders as he walked them to the bar the rest of the mercenaries had left for.

Aleah's fingers were clenched in the brown curls of Kodi's mohawk in an attempt to keep herself from swaying too far back as he walked. His hands gripped her ankles to further steady her, and though she couldn't feel the warmth of them through the leather of her boots, she knew those fingers well enough to imagine their touch.

Kodi was the epitome of dangerous. Brutal. Violent. No less so when he touched her, but she trusted him implicitly. Thinking about it too much scared her. Vulnerability in any measure was, as a general rule, a *big* no. But with Kodi ... with Kodi, she'd found physical vulnerability could be thrilling, and it often left her little more than a wobbly-limbed puddle beneath him.

Aleah wanted his hands on her more than she cared to admit in that moment, and she warred with herself silently.

We could slip into an alley.

But wouldn't it be more fun if we turned it into a game?

Games, Aleah decided, were much better suited for distraction and suppression.

Kodi stopped outside of the bar, letting Aleah slide down his shoulders and drop to the ground.

"Thanks for the ride, sir." She saluted messily.

"Find it to your satisfaction?" He grinned, grabbing her hand and pulling her to the door.

Aleah giggled, stumbling forward in an attempt to keep up with his longer stride. "I've had better."

"Perhaps I'll redeem myself later." Kodi leaned down to whisper in her ear, nipping the pointed tip before straightening.

Warmth flushed through Aleah, and she pulled ahead, greeted by the din of voices and music inside. "First round's on me, killer. Any requests?"

Kodi dropped her hand and pointed a thumb over his shoulder toward the table of Rangers at the side of the bar. "Just water for me for the rest of the night. Work in the morning, remember?"

Aleah pouted. "You should just quit and join the mercs."

Kodi arched an eyebrow, raising one wrist to show the inked aspen leaves that trailed up his forearm.

"Minor detail," she responded, waving a hand through the air.

"Minor," Kodi repeated with a roll of his eyes and a grin on his lips.

"Cam!" Aleah caught the male on his way to the bar. "Hold up, I'm headed there, too."

"I'm gonna hang out with the boys for a bit. You are absolutely welcome to join, along with the rest of the crew, of course." Kodi bowed with a flourish, nodding at Campbell as he straightened.

"Do you want to pick an extra tonight, or should I?" Aleah asked as he started to step away.

He stopped, running his teeth over his bottom lip in contemplation, before shaking his head. "Not tonight, pretty thing. I've got a more singular appetite." With a parting wink, he turned and joined the guardsmen, arms spread wide in greeting.

Aleah frowned as she walked with Campbell to the bar, but the expression didn't hold long.

"Two ales, please," Campbell called to the bartender, holding up the same amount of fingers.

Aleah followed the movements of the female working the bar with a light in her eyes that only ever meant trouble.

"He just said not tonight, Aleah," Campbell cautioned, indigo eyes flicking to the Ranger perched casually on top of a table, laughing at something one of his friends had said.

Aleah tilted her head to the side, tucking a lock of bright red hair behind her ear. "I'm just chatting with a friend," she said innocently, watching the barmaid slide Campbell his drinks.

Campbell sighed, shaking his head as he laid out some coins. "You're asking for trouble."

"Typically, yes." Aleah grinned unapologetically, leaning against the bartop and turning her attention to the fae behind the counter.

Knowing she would go against whatever he advised solely on principle, Campbell bit his cheek to keep from cautioning her again and returned with his drinks to the table where Leonidas sat with Calysta.

The bartender had delicate, leathery wings and a mess of short blonde curls that bounced when she moved. Aleah caught her attention, the mischievous grin she'd flashed Campbell turning into something much softer, but trouble still sparkled in her hazel eyes.

"What are you in the mood for tonight, sweetie?" Jessabella asked, leaning on the counter opposite Aleah. She'd been working at this bar for many years and had been a willing third to Aleah and Kodi on more than one occasion over the past year.

Aleah bit her lip, remembering the way the barmaid had looked with a light sheen of sweat over her skin, her back pressed to Kodi's front as Aleah ate her out ... the way that Kodi had later replaced the taste of Jessabella on her tongue with the taste of his blood before he'd made her come so hard she'd almost blacked out. Squeezing her thighs together, Aleah scanned the liquor bottles on the wall before answering with a flirtatious flutter of her eyelashes. "Make me something new? Sweet and fruity, clear liquor."

Jessabella's responding smile was just as playful, and a slight flush painted her cheeks as she tapped the countertop. "Anything for my favorite troublemaker." She made a show of mixing the drink, which Aleah watched with rapt attention. "Try this." She slid a glass over to Aleah.

The mercenary let out a sinful groan at the tart, berry flavor that was half an act and half just her drunkenness appreciating the artfully crafted drink. "Absolutely divine, as always." She handed over a few coppers and skipped to the table where the rest of the mercenaries sat.

Kodi's eyes tracked her across the tavern as he held a conversation with his friends. Even on a regular day, he found it impossible to cut down his awareness of her, but the past few days she'd been constantly on edge and scattered, and it worried him. When he tried to ask her if something was bothering her, she'd brushed him off and then started removing his clothes—a clear diversion tactic if there ever was one, but he took his cue not to push the issue further and settled for being as available to her as he could be.

The night out seemed to have been what she needed, though. Her cheeks flushed with both drink and happiness, and that had eased the wariness in Kodi's chest.

Until she turned to look at him, that devious glint in her eye.

He raised an eyebrow in question, a reflex that would absolutely be taken as a challenge, even if she knew he didn't intend it as such.

When she mimicked him, lips pulling up into a smirk, Kodi broke her gaze, ceding that bit of ground to communicate he wasn't trying to start something. When he lifted his eyes to meet hers again, a supplicant pull to his brow as he shook his head, Aleah only shrugged, tossing her hair over her shoulder as she turned back to her friends.

Just don't play into it, Kodi told himself. But the tiredness that was starting to tug at him warred with a desire to give in, to let Aleah have her fun.

She was always flirty; he knew that and had never minded it, and they shared partners often. So it wasn't technically unusual behavior, but he'd had a long day. He just wanted her, and then he wanted sleep. *Call it off, then,* he thought. All he had to do was walk past her and whisper *peaches*—the word they'd agreed on months ago would automatically halt any situation.

Nothing was stopping him except for her dismissal of his initial refusal. The way she seemed determined to push him served as further proof that something was wrong, and even if her refusal to talk to him about it was frustrating, he was reluctant to deny her the distraction she wanted.

As for Aleah, the alcohol in her veins removed any thought of trying to rationally work through the erratic emotions rolling through her. She was scared, but instead of acknowledging it as a fact and working through it, she wanted to ignore it.

Kodi was volatile, but she knew that he wouldn't actually hurt her, not in any permanent way. Handling her own thoughts and feelings was too much at the present, and she wouldn't have to if he fucked her senseless.

She just had to make him lose control a bit first.

Shortly after Calysta called it a night, Aleah finished her drink and sidled back up to the bar. Taking a seat at a less busy side, she smiled at Jessabella, who acknowledged her and finished helping the other customers.

"How'd that do for you?" she asked as she walked up to Aleah.

"It was the stuff of Legends," Aleah complimented, smiling brightly. "I'll take another."

"Gladly," she answered.

"Are you closing tonight?" Aleah propped her chin on her hand.

"Are you asking because you want a third?" Jessabella slid the glass over.

"Always, but Kodi's gotta turn in early."

Jessabella frowned apologetically. "Maybe next time, then."

"Wanna help me work a jealousy angle, anyway?" Aleah batted her lashes, leaning dramatically against the counter.

"Only because you ask so nicely." Jessabella laughed, blowing her a kiss before turning to help another customer.

Aleah nursed her drink at the bar, chatting with the fae whenever things slowed. There was no way Kodi would know Jessabella wasn't planning to leave with them, and Aleah felt his stare against her back throughout all of their interactions.

Until she didn't.

Aleah casually looked over her shoulder toward the table of Rangers, Kodi nowhere to be seen.

"I told you not tonight."

Kodi's whispered words against the shell of her ear sent a shiver of thrill down her spine. She turned to look at him, blinking innocently. "I don't know what you're talking about."

Kodi's bi-colored eyes searched hers, soft for only a moment before a different, darker expression took over. He dragged his teeth over his bottom lip. "Are you trying to cause a scene?"

A smile played at the corners of Aleah's mouth, and she stared dead into his eyes, giving the slightest, almost imperceptible shrug as her heart rate spiked.

"Can I get you anything, Kodi?" Jessabella asked.

The Ranger kept eye contact with Aleah. "I'm good, thanks."

Aleah turned back to the bar, opening her mouth to speak to Jessabella.

"Have a good night," he interrupted, addressing the bartender before he ducked down and hoisted Aleah over his shoulder.

She yelped, grabbing onto his shirt for support as he marched out of the bar. Kodi turned down an alley, walking until they were shrouded in shadow before setting her roughly on her feet and pushing her up against the wall.

Her back hit hard enough to force the air from her lungs in a small huff, and before she could react, Kodi had her wrists pinned to the cold stone above her head and lowered his face to hers.

Aleah's breath caught in her throat, and she tugged against his hands, knowing he wouldn't yield. She bit her lip to keep from smiling, her eyes fluttering closed at the warmth of his breath across her skin.

"What's your safe word, little merc?" Kodi growled against her mouth.

"Barmaid," Aleah replied with a devilish grin, rolling her hips against him as he took a step closer to her, pressing their bodies together.

Kodi bit her lip hard enough to draw blood. "You're just a glutton for punishment, aren't you?" He kissed her before she could reply, driving his tongue into her mouth with a possessiveness that made her dizzy with lust.

A cross between a moan and a whimper escaped her, and she brushed her tongue across his before biting it.

Kodi groaned, holding her wrists together with one hand and dragging the other roughly down her body. He squeezed her hip hard enough to bruise, forcing one of his legs between hers.

Aleah ground against his muscular thigh, panting as he moved his mouth to the base of her neck. His canines tore a small gash in her skin, blood welling to the surface, and pain twisted with the pleasure radiating from her core.

"Is this what you wanted?" he asked, letting blood trickle down her chest and pushing roughly against her. His hand slipped below her shirt to palm her breast, thumb brushing over her nipple.

"No," she breathed, tipping her head back.

Kodi released her wrists, moving his hand into her hair and gripping the nape of her neck. He shifted, untying the laces of her pants and slipping his hand down the front. His fingers slid down her center, collecting the wetness there and dragging it over her clit. "You're fucking needy, aren't you?"

"No," Aleah gasped, tilting her hips up to meet his touch as her hands flew to his shoulders, pulling him closer.

He bent to lap up the blood on her skin and brought his mouth to hers, dipping two fingers inside her and curling them against her front.

Aleah whimpered into his mouth, rocking her hips to create friction where Kodi's palm pressed against her. It took every measure of her self control not to beg him for more.

Kodi's grip tightened at the nape of her neck for a moment before sliding around to the front and applying pressure against the sides of her throat. His fingers pumped roughly into her, each time dragging heavily against that spot inside of her. "You're dripping, Aleah, so turned on from playing a tease."

"Maybe I need you to teach me a lesson, killer." Aleah was nearly breathless as she fisted one hand into the short curls at the back of Kodi's head, tugging as her tongue slid against his. Her other hand gripped his bicep, fingers digging into the muscle and feeling the flex every time he moved inside her.

"Fucking *naughty* thing." He trapped her bottom lip between his teeth, slowly pulling his head back to let his canines drag across her skin. He met her eyes, thrusting deep and swirling the heel of his hand against her clit.

Aleah's vision started to blur on the edges from the pressure against her throat, but she met his gaze, only for a moment. Then her eyes fluttered closed as she tightened around his fingers, right on the edge, his name slipping from her breathily.

And then he stilled.

"Ah, ah. We don't reward bad behavior," Kodi whispered in her ear, pulling his hand free.

Aleah whined, digging her fingers into his arms.

The Ranger peeled her hands from him and stepped away. "I'll see you tomorrow." He looked her in the eyes as he put his fingers in his mouth, licking her arousal from them with a contented sigh.

"If you don't finish this, I'll find someone else." She glared petulantly.

Kodi grinned, walking backwards down the alley. "By all means, Aleah, find someone. We both know it'll be my name on your lips when you come."

"Barmaid," she ground out, reaching to pull him back.

He spun on his heel with a laugh. "Safe words are for stopping things, not starting them."

Aleah gaped at his back, frustration boiling in her blood. "You can't just walk away!"

Without turning around, he lifted one hand in a wave as he turned the corner.

"Fucking prick." Aleah kicked an empty bottle after him. It skittered across the ground, coming to rest against the wall with a faint tink. A groan escaped her at yet another entirely unsatisfying conclusion, and she retied her pants before storming back inside the tavern.

"What's wrong with you?" Leonidas raised a brow, taking a sip of beer.

Aleah glowered at him, raising her middle finger as she slid onto the stool next to him.

He laughed. "Things with your Ranger going sour?"

"He's not my Ranger," she grumbled.

Campbell walked up behind her, draping an arm over her shoulders. "Oh, he's *definitely* your Ranger."

"Oh, I'm sorry." She turned her glare on him, shrugging off his touch. "I missed the part where you've been involved enough to *definitively* attach labels to it."

Campbell slid around her, leaning against the table between her and Leonidas and setting a cup of water in front of her. "Have either of you fucked anyone else since the mountain—*without* the other's presence or consent?"

The redhead scowled silently into her drink.

"He's your Ranger." Leonidas smiled at her disgruntlement, wrapping an arm around Campbell and pulling him closer. "And you're bleeding."

"Well, he's a fucking asshole regardless." Aleah tossed the water back before grabbing a napkin and wiping angrily at her throat.

"Are we pretending that this is new information, or?" Campbell asked cheekily.

"Did you tell him? About Do Lech?" Leonidas asked softly, reaching over Campbell to rest a comforting hand on her shoulder.

Aleah shrugged, biting her lip and suddenly very focused on the way her knee stung. She'd been skipping down the road with Merriam earlier in the night, and they'd taken a little spill. A scab was starting to form, and she pressed her finger against the raw skin.

"You can't fault him for not expecting you to be more erratic than usual right now," Campbell said.

Aleah sighed, bending to drop her forehead to the table. "I don't know why I haven't told him. He's asked, but not recently." She laughed ironically, sitting up and wiping the back of her hand where her skin had pressed against the sticky surface. "For being the cocky bastard he is, he is rudely respectful when I make it clear I don't want him to pry."

"He cares for you, Aleah. Nothing in your past is going to change that." Leonidas gave her shoulder a final squeeze before dipping another napkin into her water cup and handing it over.

"He's never known me as anything but strong." She scrubbed at her forehead and dropped the napkin to the table.

"You've never *been* anything but strong. You're the scrappiest motherfucker Nethyl has ever seen." Campbell gave her a pointed look.

Aleah shoved his shoulder, rolling her eyes. "You have to say that, you're my Cam." She pushed her fingers into her hair, a different tightness taking hold in her chest. "Do you think ..." she began, her throat closing as a wave of emotion washed away any of her former irritation. "Is not telling him pushing him away?" The possibility had never registered before, that he could eventually grow tired of her refusal to give him any emotional vulnerability. But he'd left her earlier. A *game. He was only playing the game that we insisted on starting. Right?* She twisted her fingers into the hem of her shirt.

"Hey, it's okay." Campbell leaned against her, noting the sudden change in her demeanor. "He knows you too well to be scared away by any of the stunts you pull. Tonight was mild on your spectrum."

But he said no. Her brain latched onto it, unable to recall anything else about his demeanor before he'd walked away. She took a deep breath, refusing to give in to the panic that lurked at the corners of her mind, threatening to take over. "I should apologize." Fishing a few coins from the purse at her belt, Aleah pushed the stool away from the table and hopped down.

"It can wait until tomorrow, Aleah. He'll understand." Leonidas watched her with concern, moving to follow.

She stopped him with a raised hand, forcing a smile. "It can, but Jasper left with someone hours ago and Calysta went home. I don't want to spend the rest of the night as a third wheel to all your ooey-gooey love." Some of her typical humor returned to her eyes as she teased them.

"A lack of carnage doesn't automatically qualify as ooey-gooey," Campbell retorted.

Leonidas watched her for a moment longer, finally relenting when she didn't shrink away from his gaze. "Be safe, red."

"Always am." Aleah blew them a kiss before turning from the bar.

As she walked, alone for the first time in days, Aleah contemplated the feelings that had run through her since accepting the job down south. She'd left that life behind long ago. She'd left that scared, helpless little girl behind long ago, too.

But the thought of going back there, of seeing not just her uncle, but anyone from her old life had her teetering on a strange edge she'd never encountered before.

She had grown so much, was so far past the trauma of her childhood, so why did the prospect of having to face it feel so crippling?

Kodi had asked about her scars, of course, but she'd skirted around the question every time. Something about telling him the sordid details of her past made her stomach turn uncomfortably. Not because she was worried about his perception of her. No, Kodi clearly knew there was trauma there, not even hidden so much as just in the background and out of focus.

But Aleah was *happy*.

For the first time she could remember, she was truly happy. She felt safe with Kodi. Free. She didn't want to open up that hurt from her past and mar the wonderful little thing they had together.

No romantic partner had ever fully accepted her without question or command the way he did. He'd never once made her feel as anything less than. Telling him that someone else did—someone who was supposed to love her without question—had never felt necessary. It still didn't, despite how much she knew she'd been pushing him. But her actions were her own choice, even if her childhood was not. She could apologize for them, at least.

Aleah sighed, breathing a little heavily from the trek up to the castle. The Guards at the gate waved her through without preamble—she was something of a regular between Merriam's appointment to marshal and her relationship with Kodi—and she plodded over to the Ranger's barracks.

Kodi's room was on the second floor, where the Rangers shared a kitchen, a common room, and bathrooms, but had small, individual sleeping quarters. Aleah looked around for something to throw before picking up a pinecone to toss at his window.

After the fourth hit, Kodi appeared, and he shook his head at her before disappearing.

Moments later, he came out of a door on the side of the building, wedging what looked like a boot into the jamb to keep it from closing and locking behind him. The wooden staircase on the side of the building was a fire exit, though many had questioned the sense of it being there when it was flammable and the stone building was not.

The moons bathed the courtyard in a soft glow, doing every bit of service to Kodi, who was barefoot and shirtless, with loose cotton pants hanging from his hips.

Aleah's mouth went dry when she looked at him. The desire to drag her whole face down his torso, tug his pants down, and take him into her mouth overwhelmed every other thought.

"If you're here to fuck, you'll have to come back tomorrow." Kodi smirked at her unabashed ogling.

Remembrance of her uncle and her impending trip south came rushing back, and the light guttered from her eyes. She crossed her arms over her chest, gaze dropping to the ground.

Kodi's smile fell, and he quickly crossed over to her, pulling her against his chest for a few quiet moments. "What do you need?" he asked, at a loss for what was expected of him.

"I'm sorry for pushing you earlier. I was ... upset." Aleah placed her hands on his skin, focusing on his warmth and the feel of his heartbeat under her palm.

"If you're upset with me, Aleah, learn to use your words." Kodi rested his hands on her waist.

"I'm not upset with *you*. I'm just upset in general." Aleah stayed studiously focused on her fingers as they traced patterns over his chest.

Kodi watched her blatantly avoid his gaze, brushing his thumb over her hip. "I understand if you don't want to talk to me, but you can't take it out on me, either."

Aleah's throat closed up, tears pricking at her eyes. She nodded, curling her fingers against his skin.

With a sigh, he pulled her flush to him and rested his chin on top of her head. He was unused to giving the kind of comfort he knew she needed right now. Something was tripping her up, and she was trying her hardest to ignore it. The Ranger didn't know if he should let it go or force it out of her. He just knew he would do whatever was in his power to make it better, to let her relax back into the carefree spitfire she was.

"Do you want to stay with me tonight?"

Aleah nodded, pressing against him for a moment longer before stepping back so he could take her hand and lead her inside.

She curled into a little ball in his bed, her back against his chest. Kodi wrapped himself around her, listening to her breathing even out into sleep. His arm tightened against her as he acknowledged the pain in his chest that accompanied every thought of her in distress. He'd never meant to care so much about the mercenary, but here he was, ready to burn down the whole fucking world if he thought even for a moment it would alleviate the smallest morsel of her pain.

Though he was undeniably not the greatest soldier, he still took great pride in being a Ranger. He was slowly coming to terms, however, with the fact that there was not a single thing in this world or any other that he would not sacrifice if Aleah asked him to. Somewhere along the line, Aleah and her wellbeing had become his first priority.

Something aggressively possessive and protective uncurled through his chest. He didn't know what was causing her so much distress or who had hurt her so long ago. But Legends fucking help him when he found out.

Chapter 4

Are you done?

Nine years before …

THE SUN DID LITTLE to warm Aleah as she stood at the edge of the small alley, watching the activity in the street. Fall would soon turn to winter, and a cold wind blew through the town, tugging at the cloak draped over her shoulders. Harvest was over, and the citizens of this small South Audha town were milling about, taking the time to rest before starting full preparations for winter.

Aleah didn't know the name of the town and didn't care to. She was only passing through long enough to bolster her own stores, then she would continue north, as far away from Do Lech as possible. She absentmindedly ran her fingers over her abdomen, tracing the scars scattered across the fair, freckled skin there as she watched a mother with her two small children.

One of them had pointed to a bright green apple, excitement lighting his features. The mother fondly rested her hand on his head, paying for two and handing them to her children with a loving smile.

Something cold twisted in Aleah's chest, and she averted her gaze, tugging the hood of her cloak further over her head. She stepped out into the square, glancing over the wares and goods available in nearby stalls. One vendor eyed her suspiciously as she walked past his table of antiques, and she rolled her eyes.

Aleah had grown up around all sorts of old, beautiful things. She remembered being a young child, no more than four, staring at a sparkling gem set on the fireplace mantel. Her uncle had picked her up to get a better look at it, explaining that it was glass, an heirloom passed down from many generations of fae.

She chuckled darkly, running her thumb over a puckered scab on her palm as she relived the much more recent memory of lifting the blown-glass gemstone from the mantle and throwing it to the floor, watching it shatter into hundreds of pieces. Aleah had *felt* something in that moment. For the first time in several years, she had felt something other than fear and despair, and she'd laughed as she bent to pick up a large shard, squeezing it in her fist and watching droplets of blood splatter brightly on the floor.

Shaking herself back to the present, Aleah moved along, wishing not for the first time that she'd planned this better. Those beautiful things would be worth something to these people, and she could have used them to barter for food and, more importantly, the supplies she would so desperately need if she was going to make it through the winter.

It might have been wiser to stay in the south, but the very thought of it prickled her skin and sent fear coursing through her veins. No, she needed to feel as out of their reach as possible. Out of South Eyko. Out of South Audha.

Aleah stepped up to a vendor selling various trapping equipment, pulling her cloak close around her as she surveyed their wares. The male running the stall glanced at her briefly before returning his attention to the snare he was tinkering with. Aleah was about to snag one from the table, but movement across the street caught her attention.

A tall, dark-skinned fae walked confidently through the market, black-feathered wings tucked against his back. Aleah had seen him wandering town the day before. She could tell by the way others responded to him that he wasn't a local, but he moved with purpose like he was meant to be there.

He kept a pack strapped to his back between his wings, but Aleah had seen him pull coins from a small purse at his belt as opposed to most of the town's citizens who kept their money in pockets or hanging around their necks.

Even if she was fairly certain she could steal a snare or two, she would need money for other things and was convinced it couldn't be that hard to lift a purse from a belt. So she followed him from a distance, glancing casually at the stalls she passed.

Jasper slowly made his way through the market, picking up the few supplies he would need on the trip back to Umbra the next day. Though he was well aware of the girl following him, he didn't acknowledge her. He'd seen her stalking through the town while he was conducting his business and was curious about her.

She didn't act like most street urchins, and she didn't act like she lived here, either. So he let her follow him, waiting to see what she would do.

He walked into the thick of the crowd, where people's shoulders brushed against his every so often. Sure enough, only a few steps in and he felt a tug at his belt. Not even a heartbeat later, his hand wrapped around a small wrist.

She yanked against his hold as he turned to face her, but he didn't let go. His grip was tight, but not bruising.

Fear flashed across her face when his eyes met hers, quickly replaced by anger.

Jasper had half a second to wonder if the anger was because she'd been caught or because she'd been afraid before her head swung down toward his hand.

He twisted her wrist, forcing her to spin so that her arm was held behind her body before her teeth could make contact with his skin.

She yelped, more in surprise than in pain, and Jasper grabbed her other wrist to keep her from trying to claw at him.

"Are you done?" he asked.

Aleah growled at him, thrashing for good measure.

Her response was so rough and animalistic for her small frame that he laughed, unable to hold back his amusement. Jasper released the arm that was held behind her back, letting her turn around to glare daggers at him out of bright hazel eyes.

They regarded each other, Aleah ready to slam her knee into his crotch at any moment, and Jasper completely intrigued by the untrained fire he saw in her actions.

"You're a fucking horrible thief, red," he told her.

"Let me go or I'll scream, bird boy," she hissed.

Jasper laughed again, letting her pull free. "Come on, I'll get you some food." He continued walking.

Aleah stood in the middle of the street, breathing heavily as fear, confusion, and curiosity warred inside of her.

Jasper stopped, looking back at her. "Are you hungry or not?"

Aleah curled her hands into fists, contemplating for only a moment longer before deciding to follow him.

He led her to an inn, holding the door open for her. "Can you send supper up to my room tonight, please?" he asked the innkeeper, who nodded, jotting something down on a notepad. Jasper moved up the stairs, using a key to enter a room near the end of the hallway.

"Food should be here shortly. You're welcome to stay here if you don't have a place to sleep tonight."

As soon as the door was shut, Aleah's heart started pounding, unease crawling over her skin. What was she doing? Was she trapped? What did this male want with her? Why was she stupid enough to follow him?

She scrambled over to the window, pressing her back to the wall beside it as she watched Jasper.

He gave her a funny look, but there was nothing nefarious in his eyes or in his posture. He removed his pack, setting it on the small table by the bedside, and sat to unlace his boots, placing them neatly at the side of the bed.

A knock sounded at the door, and he opened it, retrieving a tray of food before locking it again. Jasper stood, one hand in his pocket, and held the plate out toward her.

Aleah, still unsure of his intentions, crept slowly forward. She reached out, pulling a flank steak from the plate before retreating to the window. She slid down the wall, a loud growl rumbling from her belly as the smell of the meat wafted around her, setting her mouth watering.

Aleah tore into the meat without finesse, grease coating her cheeks as she quickly chewed and swallowed.

Jasper laughed, tossing a bread roll to her.

She bared her teeth at him like a feral cat, but scooped the roll from where it had landed on the floor next to her feet.

"Take it easy there, red. You'll make yourself sick eating that fast."

Aleah glared at him, but continued to eat at a more normal pace, settling into her place by the window. She watched distrustfully as Jasper sat on the bed, folding his legs in front of him and laying out a set of gleaming knives.

He dug a whetting stone from his pack and went to work, honing each blade. When she'd finished her food, Aleah wiped the back of her hand over her face, pulling her knees up to her chest as she watched him. Her wide, hazel eyes tracked each of his movements, but he never once looked up to meet her wary gaze.

Satisfied with the condition of his weapons, Jasper wrapped them back up, leaving one knife lying on the blanket while he stored the others with the whetting stone in his pack. He picked the remaining knife up, tossing it into the air. The blade gleamed in the light as it flipped end over end. Catching it by the hilt, Jasper gave it one final flip, clasping the flat of the blade between his first two fingers and thumb.

Finally, he raised his silver eyes to Aleah, extending his arm toward her.

Aleah searched his face, narrowing her eyes.

Jasper shrugged, tossing the knife towards the end of the bed. He grabbed a book from the nightstand and settled against the headboard, his wings splayed to either side as he read.

Aleah watched him for a moment longer before darting forward to grab the knife, scurrying backward until her shoulder blades hit the wall with a dull thud.

Jasper chuckled at the sound, but he turned a page without looking up.

Aleah wanted to threaten him for finding her amusing, but she bit her tongue. She knew nothing about this male except what she'd observed in watching him, which was admittedly not much.

She shifted her hold on the knife, wetting her lips, entire body tensed.

"Bathroom is through that door to your left, if you need it." Jasper flipped another page.

Several minutes went by before Aleah slowly stood, her knees cracking and knuckles white from her grip on the knife. She kept her eyes on Jasper as she scooted sideways into the bathroom, closing and locking the door.

With a shaky breath, she set the knife on the counter and drank straight from the faucet, rubbing at her teeth with a finger before finally taking a moment to look at her reflection in the mirror.

She almost laughed at how wild she looked. The red of her hair was dull from how dirty she was, and dark circles hung beneath her eyes, her cheeks hollow from hunger. Even filthy and half-starved, there was a gleam in her eyes that had never been there before, something that spoke of fight and fire.

Aleah placed her palms on the counter, tilting her head to the side as she regarded herself. The girl who had been sheltered from the world was nowhere to be seen. The girl who had suffered at the hands of those who were supposed to protect her—the girl with sad, scared eyes—was gone.

Staring at herself in the bathroom of an inn somewhere in South Audha, Aleah knew that she would never be that quiet, timid girl again. She would never again allow herself to become a victim.

With that resolution settling inside of her, Aleah turned on the tap to the shower and stripped off her dirty clothes. Washing her hair with soap and hot water felt like a luxury. The water almost burned against her skin, but she relished it, watching the dirt and grime from weeks on the road wash down the drain. She dried off, looking with distaste at her travel-stained clothing. But she didn't have much of a choice.

After she dressed, she picked up the knife and ran the point along one of the lines of her palm, watching its path as a shiver ran up her spine from the tickle of the metal against her flesh. She contemplated staying in the bathroom behind the locked door, but there was no window. If the winged male were to leave, she'd have no way of knowing.

Which wouldn't matter except for whoever came into the room after he left might not be so kind to her. She had a knife, sure, but how many people could she fight her way through with no training?

It was best to be able to keep an eye on things and have multiple exit points, Aleah finally decided, and slowly, she cracked open the door.

Jasper remained where he'd been when she left, so she pushed the door open further and returned to her spot beside the window, holding the knife in her lap and resting her chin on her knees.

Unease still coursed through her, but she was tired, and her belly was full for the first time in days. When it became too much effort to keep her eyelids from falling closed, she let them stay there, intently listening. If Jasper shifted from the bed, she'd be able to hear and bring her weapon to the ready.

Jasper's gaze flicked to the feral child curled on the floor of his room. She'd fought it for a while, but he could tell from her breathing that she'd fallen asleep. Her brow was still pulled together in a glare, but one of her arms had fallen from her lap, and her head listed to the side.

A spark of fondness bloomed in the mercenary's chest as he watched her. Her small frame held more fight than many fully grown males he'd encountered, and it filled him with equal parts admiration and sorrow.

Nobody grew that level of ferocity so young without necessity.

Setting his book aside, Jasper stood, grabbing a pillow and blanket from the bed and walking over to Aleah. Squatting in front of her, he set the pillow on the floor and slowly, gently, guided her to lie down.

She didn't stir, the exhaustion in her body too heavy.

As he carefully pulled the knife from her hands and draped the blanket over her, he wondered what had happened in her short life to elicit such a violent response from her at any small act of kindness. Something about her mannerisms made him doubt that she'd been raised on the streets, and she was far too clumsy a thief to have made it this long in life alone.

Jasper suppressed the sudden urge to smooth a hand over her hair, not wanting to wake her. He could only imagine how she might respond if she woke up to him looming over her, the knife he'd given her plucked from her sleeping grasp.

Sitting back on his heels, Jasper set the weapon next to where one of her hands had fallen, close enough that if she stretched out her fingers, she could grab the hilt, but not where she was in danger of accidentally cutting herself in her sleep.

He stood, walking to the bathroom to get ready for bed. As he washed up, he thought about the girl. When he'd invited her back to the inn with him, he hadn't had any further thought other than faint amusement at her antics, respect for her determination, and knowledge that he could at least give her a meal for having the gumption to try to steal from him.

But the more he saw of her, though she'd barely said three sentences to him, the more he realized that she was on her own in a way she wasn't used to. She was feisty and was learning to be scrappy, but she wouldn't make it out there without someone to guide her along the way.

He'd recently purchased an empty building in Umbra, intending to set it up as a home base of sorts. He had plenty of room, and he could teach the girl, give her a chance at something better.

What am I doing? I'm no babysitter. Jasper ran a hand down his face, shaking his head. There were hundreds of orphans in Sekha, hundreds of traumatized half-fae children trying to navigate a world that had despised their existence for so long. He couldn't take them all in. He didn't *want* to take them all in, and her fate was already better than some.

As Jasper tucked himself in for the night, he decided that he would offer the girl one final meal in the morning, then he would head back home and leave her to her fate. *She's not my responsibility. I've done enough.*

Aleah startled awake, her eyes flying open and her heart pounding against her ribcage. Her fingers brushed against something smooth and cool, and she instinctively pulled back from it, shooting into an upright position.

The blanket fell from her shoulders, her eyes catching the gleam of light against the blade of the knife. She grabbed it, holding it out in front of her as she scanned the room in the soft gray light of pre-dawn.

Jasper was asleep in the bed, the blankets pooled around his waist. He slept on his side, black-feathered wings stretched out behind him. Aleah watched the gentle rise and fall of his chest for a moment before her gaze traveled over the rest of his torso.

Powerful cords of muscle ran beneath his skin, but other than a brief recognition of the fact that he was incredibly strong, the cut of his body went unnoticed.

Aleah's eyes traced his scars.

Some were raised, jagged lines, others a pinkish color that contrasted against the dark brown of his skin.

Without thinking, Aleah's fingers slipped under her shirt, tracing the scars across her own body. She wondered where his had come from, if he'd earned them in a fight or learned to fight because of them.

She sank back to the floor, letting her head rest against the pillow. The idea of earning scars had never occurred to her before, but it held appeal. Still gripping the knife, she let her eyes fall closed, slowly drifting back to sleep.

The smell of cooked meat brought her back to consciousness, and she opened her eyes.

Jasper sat at the small table against the far wall of the room, eating some sort of breakfast sandwich. "There's an extra if you'd like it," he said when he noticed her stare.

Aleah sat up, worrying her lip between her teeth before walking over, reaching a hand out.

Jasper leveled his gaze at her, pausing her in her tracks. "Assuming you understand civility, if you want breakfast, eat at the table."

Aleah glowered at him, but complied, plopping down into the chair across from him and setting down her knife. Jasper stood to pack his things, letting her eat in silence. When she was finished, he waited for her eyes to find him before tossing something at her.

She caught it, turning it in her hands to examine the two pieces of supple leather that had been sewn together, a loop on one end. A smile pulled at her lips as she realized what it was.

"That dagger will cut almost anything when you put a little pressure behind it. I guess you might have assumed as much since you haven't tucked it into your belt yet."

Aleah was already looping the sheath around her belt, tucking the knife into it. "What do you want for it?"

Jasper blinked, his eyebrows raising.

Aleah ran her hands through her hair, tying it up at the top of her head. "I'm not stupid. It's a nice knife. Nobody gives stuff like that away for free."

Jasper shrugged, turning to resume packing his things. "I have several."

Aleah grit her teeth, folding her arms across her chest. The thought of giving up the illusion of safety a weapon provided chilled her, but she didn't want to owe this male anything more than she already did for his kindness.

"Look, if you really want to do something for me in return, keep yourself alive, red."

Aleah blinked, following him from the room without really thinking about it. "What does it matter to you if I live or not?"

"I suppose it doesn't, but you're a fighter. The world needs more of us." Jasper walked down the stairs of the inn, setting the key to the room on the counter and waving to the innkeeper before heading out into the street.

Aleah drew the hood of her cloak over her head when she stepped over the threshold, mostly on muscle memory. "I don't understand." She glared at his back, picking up her pace to match his long strides.

Jasper laughed, looking down at her. "You weren't born a street rat. Either something forced you out here, or—and this is the option I'd put my money on—you chose this for yourself. Now, that could mean you're just a bratty kid playing at runaway, but the more likely scenario is that sleeping in alleys and scrounging through dumpsters for food was a more appealing life than whatever you were dealing with before."

Aleah's fingers folded over the edges of her cloak, her eyes on her feet.

"It takes fight to choose survival when survival also means being scared and cold and hungry," Jasper finished.

Aleah didn't respond, but kept walking by his side. She didn't even notice when he changed his gait, making it easier for her to keep up.

It wasn't until they'd left the city behind and were deep in the forest that Aleah realized she was following him, and she stuttered to a halt.

Jasper kept walking, aware that she was no longer at his side, but not responding to it.

He'd gotten several paces ahead of her before she started walking again. "Where are you going?" she called, concern lacing her voice.

"Home," he answered simply. "Where are *you* going?"

Aleah swallowed against the lump in her throat. *Anywhere but home.* "North."

Jasper didn't reply, just kept walking, knowing Aleah followed at a distance and hoping she continued to do so.

Chapter 5

She's tenacious

A GENTLE SERIES OF chimes sounded across the second floor of the Ranger barracks, signaling the start of first shift. Kodi rolled over and buried his face in Aleah's hair. She always smelled like strawberries, sweet and bright, and he took a moment to soak in her warmth, feeling the soft rise and fall of her chest. After the first few nights she'd stayed with him, she'd quickly learned that the chiming meant nothing to her and started sleeping right through it.

Reluctantly, Kodi slid out of bed with a stretch before donning his uniform. Once he was dressed, he left a cup of water and a couple small capsules for headache relief on the nightstand and dropped a kiss to Aleah's temple. "Have a good day, little merc," he murmured, a fond smile passing over his lips before he departed quietly.

The soft click of the latching door made Aleah stir, her face crumpling into a frown with the recognition that she was alone, but her head hurt, and she was still exhausted, so she snuggled deeper into Kodi's blankets and fell back asleep.

When she next woke, a line of drool trailed from her mouth to the pillow, and she grimaced, wiping her cheek with the heel of her hand. She lay there for a moment, blinking sleep from her eyes and deciding whether or not she was ready to be awake. Spying the water beside the bed, she crawled forward to take a few sips and down the pills. *You're too good to us, Ko,* she thought. As she drank, her mind tipped back to a drunken conversation she'd had with Merriam years before about internal monologues.

"I dunno, I just always refer to myself in the second person, like I'm talking to someone else instead of myself," Merriam had said.

"You never use multiples? For me, it's always we, us, our. Maybe that just means I'm crazy," Aleah had offered with a laugh.

"Multiples actually makes a lot of sense, actually." Merriam had paused to hiccup. "Like, there's you, but you're also talking to the child you left behind when you decided to become you."

After frowning for a thoughtful moment, Aleah had promptly decided that things were getting too introspective and steered the conversation another direction.

The door opened, jarring Aleah from the memory.

"Good morning, my little bundle of trouble," Kodi greeted, striding across the room and tilting her face up to kiss her.

"I haven't brushed my teeth yet," she told him.

Ignoring the statement, he pushed her back onto the bed, crawling over her and burying his face in her neck to hide his smile, but she could feel it against her skin.

"What's got you so perky? Shouldn't you be working?" she asked with a giggle, shrugging her shoulder against the tickle of his hair.

"I've been reassigned." He sat up on his elbows, eagerness in his mismatched eyes.

She put a hand on either side of his face, his joy bleeding into her. "Well, spit it out already, killer."

"I'm going to Do Lech." He grinned.

Aleah blinked, pushing him to the side so she could sit up and face him. Hearing the city's name was like a cold plunge, but it was immediately followed by the recognition that Kodi would be with her. For seven days each way, she'd have Merriam, and she'd have him, and that filled her with a giddy warmth that made her fingers tingle. "You're going to … You're coming?" she asked, a slow smile spreading across her face.

"Rov gave me the assignment this morning."

Aleah squeaked, slapping her hands to her mouth. "Is *Rovin* going?"

Kodi nodded, already understanding the glimmer in her hazel eyes.

"I need to go see Mer." She jumped up to pull her pants and boots from where she'd discarded them the night before. She squeaked again, turning to straddle Kodi with her pants clutched in one hand. "You're going." Her cheeks hurt, she was smiling so hard.

"I'm going," Kodi affirmed, squeezing her hips. Her simple happiness that he'd be with her filled his heart to bursting, and he was almost overwhelmed with the desire to crush her to his chest and devour her.

Unable to contain her energy, Aleah did a little full body shimmy before leaning forward to kiss him; then she was up, shoving her legs into her pants and fumbling with her boots. When she was finished, she moved to stand between his legs, looping her arms over his shoulders. He tilted his face up to look at her, his own arms around her waist. "This has been the best possible news."

"I won't disagree," he replied as she bent to kiss his forehead. "Now get out of here before I decide I need you in my bed all day."

She cocked an eyebrow. "Those are big words from someone who wouldn't finish what he started last night."

A hungry gleam lit Kodi's eyes as he met her stare. "Do you have things you want to get done today, little merc, or do you want me to take that challenge?"

Tempted, Aleah bit her lip. But then she remembered Merriam, and tamped down her lust. "Okay, okay, I'm gone," she acquiesced, taking a few steps back. "But maybe come by the merc house tonight?"

"Why? Is Campbell planning to cook venison?"

Aleah rolled her eyes, clicking her tongue against her teeth.

"I'll be there," he promised, chasing her from the room with a well-placed swat to her ass. Still smiling, Aleah headed toward the castle in search of the marshal, only slightly sick with her conflicting feelings regarding the trip south.

After sorting things out with Merriam, Aleah made her way back down into the city, the contract Merriam had given her to explain the mercenaries' presence in Do Lech tucked safely into a pocket. Stopping by a butcher shop, she picked out a few steaks, cradling the package to her chest as she continued home.

Her earlier, simplistic happiness at being able to spend time with people she cared about was slowly dissipating, overshadowed by reality. Merriam knew the details of Aleah's past and the years she'd spent suffering her uncle's abuse and had forced Aleah to actually face the fact that Merriam and Kodi would be staying at the estate she'd formerly called home, with the people who had been her family. She swallowed roughly, not wanting to think about it, but at the same time unable to consider anything else.

With a frustrated huff, she picked up her pace, not wanting to be alone and needing the distraction of other people. Aleah preferred to pretend that whatever had happened in her past had happened to some other girl. Someone weaker, more vulnerable, and so far different from who Aleah was that those things would never be able to happen to *her*. She chewed the inside of her cheek, growing more unsettled with each step.

The evening she'd spent with Kodi had calmed her, and she forced her focus on him and the dependency she'd unwittingly developed there. He'd become so entirely important to her in such a short amount of time, and she wasn't sure when he'd crossed the line from being a fun fuck to being …

What was he, even? Someone she was obsessed with. Someone she would kill for. Someone she felt possessive of, even though seeing him take his pleasure from another heated her blood in a delicious way. Someone who was *hers* in a way that no one ever had been.

She immediately pushed the last thought away. Claiming him outright felt too intimate, which she knew was ridiculous. Kodi was etched into the very makeup of her being regardless of how much she wanted to deny it.

But love wasn't safe, not for her. She'd learned very early on that love was merely a sentiment people used to manipulate her. People only said they loved her when they needed something from her. Love made her wary, put her on edge, like she needed to be careful about what was coming next and pay closer attention to what was happening around her and what reaction was expected from her.

Kodi was the opposite of that. Everything about him made her feel safe and enveloped in a way that she'd never even dreamed possible.

Giving herself over to him was thrilling, because just as she knew he was capable of hurting her in a million different ways, she knew that he never would. He read her body like her desires had been written right into the fabric of his mind.

Even the way he talked to her made her feel seen and valued beyond measure. He'd ask her for advice and talk through strategy with her and listen to her plans for her own jobs, offering input and fresh perspective.

Every single thing about that cocksure bastard melted her, and the thought of losing or marring what they had in any way made her want to tear something apart with her teeth.

That feral fear started to claw its way through her, and though it couldn't be more different than the paralyzing fear that accompanied thoughts of her family, it was just as overwhelming, and she bit her tongue hard enough to draw blood before she could start to spiral.

Clutching the parcel of meat closer to her chest, she swallowed the tang of iron that filled her mouth, sucking against the small wound on her tongue until it quickly clotted. "Mer and Rov, though," she whispered with a small smile, turning her thoughts back to her friend—a much safer course of thought. Teasing Merriam about whatever thing had been going on between her and Rovin was a welcome distraction from Aleah's own emotional turmoil. It would be seven days on the road that Aleah would be able to pick at her, and she knew Kodi would more than happily corral Rovin as well.

Aleah hadn't pushed very hard, respectful of Merriam's grief, but she had purposefully organized events that would put Merriam and Rovin together. She couldn't help it—the thought of her best friend being with Kodi's best friend was too fun not to entertain. It had taken only a single report of him talking about her skill when slaying demons in that cave for Aleah to latch on to the idea of nudging them together.

So, she occupied her thoughts with their bar games from the night before, examining every little interaction between them rather than thinking about her meltdown at the end of the night.

She burst through the back door of the merc house, heading straight for the kitchen. "I'm home!" she called. Silence greeted her as she stored the meat in the icebox. After a quick lap around the house, the office upstairs and the training room both empty, she set up on the floor of the mushroom to sharpen her knives.

Campbell was the first to return, and she immediately latched onto him, helping him prep for supper. She was bursting at the seams to talk to someone about what had happened with Merriam and Rovin after the others had left, wanting to get another perspective, but held her tongue. She'd managed to refrain from discussing her matchmaking scheme with anyone other than Kodi so far, and she was immensely proud of herself for it. She knew Merriam well enough to know that if the others started teasing her about Rovin before she was ready, she'd dig her heels in even harder and refuse to admit she could ever even possibly like him just based on principle. So she talked instead about whatever job Campbell had worked that day and what else he had lined up until Leonidas came in, and she accosted him with a knife throwing competition in the training room.

But after only a couple of rounds, he handed off his set of knives. "I've got some paperwork I want to sort out before it gets too late."

Aleah replaced both sets where they belonged and followed him from the room. "What kind of paperwork? Anything I can help with?"

Jasper was just coming down the hall, raindrops glistening in the twisted locs of his hair and sliding down the black feathers of his wings. "It's pouring out there," he needlessly remarked.

"Oh good, you're home. It's your turn for avoidance duty," Leonidas called to him, wrapping his arms around Aleah's shoulders and walking her over to the fae.

Aleah ducked from his grasp, spinning around to slap at his chest. "Dick." She laughed.

Leonidas caught her hands easily, looking at Jasper with one eyebrow raised to emphasize his point.

"I talked to Mer today," Aleah said, tugging free and falling over onto the couch. She'd left the contract on the floor next to her whetting kit, which was still strewn about. She reached down to pluck up the paper, holding it out to Jasper. "We've been hired to keep my dear grandparents honest and check out all the potential locations for Molli's train station."

"Oh?" Jasper walked over, stepping over the assortment of knives to grab the paper. "Night recon. Nice." A small smile played across his lips. "I'm assuming our marshal knows better than to expect you to be setting foot in the city?"

Aleah glared before rolling to the floor to clean up her mess. "Who's to say I won't be?"

Jasper didn't even dignify the question with a response, silver eyes reading over the details.

"It's not like it's anything you're not capable of by yourself," she muttered.

"And how much of your cut will I be getting for doing all of the work?" Jasper tossed the contract to the table and settled onto the couch.

"Meh, just let our accountant figure out those details." Aleah waved him off and placed her tools and knives next to it, pushing to her feet. "I'm going to see if Cam needs any help."

Jasper and Leonidas watched her disappear into the kitchen.

"She's going to be a handful," Leonidas said.

"I was hoping she would back out, to be honest," Jasper admitted.

Leonidas huffed a laugh at that. "She'd never risk her reputation that way. Besides, maybe this will be good for her. It's been years, and she's never really faced what she went through."

"I know," Jasper sighed, running a hand over the back of his neck. "But she was so young, Leo. And when I first met her … the way every little kindness made her suspicious and on edge … all of her formative years were spent in abuse. That kind of trauma is ingrained deep."

"It's impressive how much she's still managing to deny that it affects her, even while actively planning."

"Only Aleah," Jasper said with a shake of his head and a sad smile. "She's tenacious in most things, even denial."

A knock sounded from the back door, and Aleah came barreling out of the kitchen so fast, she startled Panic. He screeched once from his perch, feathers ruffled in distaste. "I invited Kodi for supper," she tossed over her shoulder as she ran down the hallway.

"I guess they made up, then," Leonidas remarked.

"They were fighting?" Jasper was mildly intrigued.

Leonidas shrugged. "She was either fighting him or fighting herself. Probably both." Then he disappeared upstairs to the office.

Aleah returned to the mushroom, Kodi following with a drenched cloak held in one hand. Rather than walk it up to her room, Aleah grabbed it and hung it from Panic's perch.

The falcon took it as an offense, narrowing a golden glare at Kodi before flying up the stairs after Leonidas.

"You're going to make him hate me," Kodi complained.

Aleah tsked. "Better you than me! It's nice no longer being his least favorite."

Kodi rolled his eyes at her, before turning to greet Jasper and joining him on the couch. "Have you heard any of the rumors of the drug trade growth out west?" he asked, and they talked about different regulations and responses to potential issues regarding the matter until the food was ready.

Everyone was seated in the mushroom, just starting to dig in, when Calysta stormed in, water streaming from her hair and skirt sticking to her legs, the olive-green flesh dotted with goosebumps as she shivered.

"Why is mountain rain so *cold?*" the nymph grumbled, pointed teeth chattering and arms held stiffly at her sides as she continued to mutter about temperatures and numb toes on her way upstairs for a warm shower.

When she returned, hair wrapped in a towel, she stopped in the kitchen to grab the bowl of vegetables Campbell had made her before sinking down next to Aleah.

"Wanna share my room tonight?" the redhead offered with an apologetic glance at Kodi.

Calysta sighed, lifting a forkful of steaming asparagus to her mouth. "It stopped just before I made it home, and it looked like the skies were clearing. But thank you."

Leonidas dug into his pants pocket, passing a rolled note to the nymph. "This came for you at the aviary earlier today."

"Oh?" Calysta took the note, tied with a thin rope of dried bramble. She slid her thumb over the knot before breaking it free and opening it. "It's from Novi." Calysta hoped the small smile on her lips covered the worry that slowly churned through her stomach. "I'll write back tomorrow, but if you're gone, I'll just run it next door to Horscha," she told Leonidas before rolling the paper back up and tucking it into a pocket of her dress.

Chapter 6
Nymphy aloofness

Novi's letter made Calysta nervous. There was no reason for it to, really. She and the other wood nymph wrote to each other a few times a year and had been one another's closest companions for over a century.

Close in nymph terms, at least. Like most of their kind, Novi preferred solitude. Calysta, however, had found herself in the middle of the most rambunctious, loud, and close-knit group of people in all of Sekha. And she would happily die for any of them.

After supper, Calysta climbed up to her rooftop garden, the late summer air cool against her skin from the earlier storm. Now that it had passed, only the slightest breeze brushed through the night, and the smell of damp earth permeated the air.

Despite Aleah's impending trip south and her increasing, unacknowledged uneasiness about it, the world around Calysta felt calm and centered. She relished times like these. They were all taking on various low-risk jobs, home every night for supper, and back into a typical routine. The peril of the previous summer felt long behind them, and even though Merriam no longer held the title of mercenary, they were still all here, the little family they'd cultivated thriving as much as they ever had.

Calysta smiled up at the moons, starlight sparkling in her ink-black eyes as she sank to the ground, her back resting against a raised garden bed. Closing her eyes, she splayed her fingers out, letting her magic wander through the plants, feeling their energy and coaxing it further. With a sigh, she dug the small note from her pocket and unrolled it against her knee, the crisp cream of the paper standing out against her olive-green skin.

I miss you. Come south before the turn of autumn. Tides are rising.

They'd stopped signing their letters to each other ages ago, but the tight, elegant scrawl was as familiar as her own name. The close of the message was typical. *Tides are rising. Flowers are blooming. Moons are waxing.* Nature was running its course, and all was well.

It was those three little words at the beginning that knotted Calysta's stomach. The folk were not especially sentimental. Novi wasn't simply expressing an emotion. That statement came with a subtext that may as well have been written in bold and announced by a courier. If Calysta's presence was missed, it was because there was a reason her friend needed her there, something they wanted her to be present for.

After ripping the note in half and tossing the pieces into a planter, Calysta placed her palms down on either side of her and let her magic slip free to fortify the bed of moss beneath her. Then she collapsed back, pink hair spilling out around her as she stared up at the sky.

She already knew she would go. Her friend had asked for her, and she would not deny that request, but she wanted time to settle her nerves before she told the others. She could see Novi, and she could help in Do Lech, and neither of those things had to mean that anything was changing or important things were happening.

With a final sigh, Calysta rolled onto her side, tucking her hands beneath her chin, and let sleep claim her.

She woke with the sun the next morning, stretching luxuriously before sitting up and plucking bits of moss from her hair. After picking a couple of peppers and a melon, the nymph headed inside, bare feet padding softly on the wood floorboards of the hallway.

Leonidas met her at the base of the stairs, taking the melon from her grasp and leading her into the kitchen. "How was moonbathing?" he asked, like he did almost every time they spent the morning together.

Calysta smiled, her pointed teeth dimpling her lower lip. "Positively lovely," she answered, rinsing off the peppers in the sink and setting them on the counter.

Campbell came down next, stopping below Panic's perch and scratching the falcon's chest. "Anyone feel like a run this morning?"

"I'd love to join you," Calysta replied.

Leonidas wrinkled his nose. "Not in the slightest. But take Panic with you—he could use the stretch."

"You heard the man, Pan. Let's go." Campbell made a clicking noise out of the side of his mouth, alerting the falcon to follow him, and he and Calysta were off.

Everyone was up and finishing a workout in the training room when they returned, and by the time they'd all gathered for breakfast, her nerves from the night before had dissipated with the morning fog that settled over the mountains.

"Novi asked me to visit," she announced without preamble.

Aleah's spoonful of oatmeal stopped halfway to her mouth, a smile stretching her freckled cheeks. "Does that mean you're coming with us?"

"Indeed, it does." Calysta smiled back.

"Will you be staying with us? I can go make changes to the accommodations we have planned," the redhead offered excitedly.

Calysta shook her head. "No need. I'll be spending most of my time among the folk. I'll definitely stop by and visit, though. I have a feeling I'll need a reprieve," she said with a light, musical laugh.

"Yeah, you've lost a bit of that nymphy aloofness over the years," Aleah teased.

The wood nymph smiled, warmth filling her as the others picked up the light banter amongst each other. *This is right*, she thought. *And nothing will change.*

Chapter 7
A truly terrifying creature

Two days after Calysta decided to go with Jasper and Aleah, the three of them packed up and joined the official envoy to head south. Aleah had tried her best to convince Campbell and Leonidas to join them, but Leonidas insisted that he couldn't leave his birds for that long, and they were both eager to have the house to themselves for once.

Though Aleah had been brash in Umbra, acting on every impulse to keep herself from having to dwell on the trip, she became more reserved the closer they got to Do Lech, barely leaving Jasper's side in a childish reversion of perceived safety.

Kodi had tried to pull her out of it at first. She wouldn't talk about what had her on edge, he knew that, so he tried his best to distract her instead. Early their third morning on the road, just as the first rays of sun were peeking over the horizon, he slipped up to where she slept, sprawling next to her on his belly. "Hey, slumber-goose," he whispered, gently digging his elbow into her arm.

A small noise somewhere between a whine and groan crawled up Aleah's throat, and she tossed her arms over her head in a stretch before opening her eyes. "You lost, Ranger?" She smiled, voice husky with sleep.

"As a general rule? Never." He lowered his voice. "I have gossip for you."

Aleah wriggled closer. "That's one way to make a girl happy in the morning."

"Rov's definitely picking up feelings for our demonslayer. I guess Eskar said something rude about her last night, and he picked a fight with her about it in front of some of the other Guard," he whispered secretively, aware that Merriam was sleeping not too far away.

"He did not." Aleah's eyes widened with delight, and she struggled to keep her voice low.

"He's fighting it, but he'll find an excuse to stay close to her in Do Lech; I'll put money on it."

Aleah's smile twitched, almost dropping, and a faraway look glazed her eyes at the mention of the city. She pressed her face against Kodi's arm, biting above his elbow as she forced down the panic rising within her.

The sudden change in her demeanor both confused and worried him, and she only got worse as they traveled. He didn't care that she was clinging to Jasper, not in the sense that he was jealous, at least. He was thankful that the mercenary was there, knew he'd protect Aleah at all costs, but the clear fear that she was trying to hide ate at him.

Someone had hurt her, that much was obvious. Every time he saw her chewing at her nails as they rode or tucked beneath Jasper's wing around the fire at night, her scars flashed through his mind, and his magic would surge up and press against him, fueled by anger and a promise for revenge.

It wasn't just anger and possession, though. He loved her, and the fact that he couldn't communicate that to her without sending her into a deeper spiral was driving him half-insane.

Kodi had confessed his love once, and it had been the only time she'd ever used a safe word with him. He'd thought it was the knife at first. He'd drawn a pretty line of broken skin across her collarbone—shallow enough that her half-fae blood could heal it without scarring—and the noise she'd made when he licked it ... Legends save him. It almost sent him over the edge. He had known he loved her before then, but he couldn't hold it back in that moment. Said it right against her skin, and almost immediately she called a stop.

He'd never said it again, confident that she knew the depth of his feelings for her and would address it in her own time, when she was comfortable. He understood that something in her trauma caused fear in response to spoken intimacy, and it wasn't up to him to push her past that.

Between the responsibilities he had to the Guard, he kept an eye on her throughout the trip, not wanting to force himself into her space, but making sure he stayed close if she ever did need anything. It wasn't until their last night on the road that Aleah finally told him her story, her voice quiet and more unsteady than he'd ever heard her as she recounted the abuse she endured throughout her childhood.

Indignation surged through Kodi's veins, stealing the breath from his lungs. He curled his hands into fists to keep them from shaking, Aleah's warm body pressed to his side the only thing keeping him from leaping to his feet in a rage. "He will die for ever having laid a finger on you," he promised.

Aleah shook her head, huddling deeper into him. "You don't understand, Ko. Taking out a Kinbriar is like taking out a Stonebane. There's too much history and power there. The repercussions ..."

Kodi snorted despite himself. "You're telling me Mollian couldn't have him charged with child abuse? That if you—" He stopped, understanding dawning on him. "You won't testify."

"I'm not that kid anymore," Aleah said, shoulders hunched. "I've built a reputation for myself in Umbra as this fearless, untouchable mercenary. People twice my size see me as dangerous—would rather slap their own mothers than get on my bad side." She smiled a little at that, tipping her face up to meet Kodi's eyes. "If my past became public knowledge—and it would have to in order for anything against my uncle to stick—then when people looked at me, they would see that small, scared child who'd been completely helpless, worthless even to her own family." Tears lined her hazel eyes, shimmering in the firelight. "That's not me. And I refuse to ever give anyone a reason to see me that way." A small tremor traveled down her spine, and Kodi wrapped his arms around her and pulled her against his chest.

"You are worth *everything*, Aleah," he said, his own throat tight with emotion.

"Being so close to it all again, it ..." She swallowed, searching for the words to explain what was going on in her head. "I'd never been afraid of anything before my uncle, and I haven't been afraid of anything since. The thought of ever seeing him again ... it ... I hate how much it terrifies me, but it does. I can't shake this thought that if he found out I was still alive, he'd kill me. Or worse, find some way to dismantle everything I have and leave me weak and alone. And you know the worst part? I'm disgusted with myself for that fear. I'm a fucking assassin. I've fought literal demons and *won*. But at the thought of some classist prick who probably hasn't even held a sword in years, I'm ready to hide under my blankets and piss myself. I hate it. I hate it so much, but I know that if I even felt his eyes on me again, I'd freeze."

Kodi didn't know what to say or how to comfort her, but he felt her pain as sharply as if it were his own. And through it all, his anger grew, solidifying into something with sharp spines and gnashing teeth. He ran a hand over her hair, a much more tender feeling swelling up inside him so quickly his fingers trembled. "The fact that you've only ever had one fear your whole life makes you a truly terrifying creature," he whispered against her temple.

"You flatter me, killer." She nuzzled his neck because pulling back, sniffling a little as she reeled in the heavy flood of emotions. "We're being monitored."

Kodi looked to where Jasper leaned against a tree, watching them. When the Ranger's gaze met his, he walked over, raising a hand before Aleah could speak.

"Don't worry, I'm not here to check on you," he told her, a slight tilt to his lips, then he looked at Kodi, folding his arms over his chest. "I actually wanted to talk to you."

Kodi's eyes widened in surprise. "Why?"

"To let you know I understand better than most what it's like to see things—to *know* things—and be unable to do anything about it. That sort of rage is hard to leash, but sometimes it's necessary."

Kodi grit his teeth, looking into the fire. Aleah's hand found his, squeezing it tight, and he gripped hers back like a lifeline.

"I know you have a lot to mull over and sit with right now, but promise me that you'll find me before you do anything rash. I can help you. You don't have to shoulder anything alone, not when it's this heavy," Jasper said.

Kodi swallowed, looking first at Aleah, the firelight dancing across her freckled cheeks and reflecting only the amber in her hazel eyes. *Legends, I fucking love you.* He nearly choked on the words, even more so now that he understood why she didn't want to hear them, what love had meant to her in the past. So he flicked his gaze to Jasper, nodding once, and as the mercenary's cool silver gaze met his, he felt the depth of the offer, and it fed the beast that still circled in Kodi's chest.

Chapter 8

Hey, buck

Four years before …

CAMPBELL WAS SITTING AT a bar eating a sandwich of shredded chicken that he knew without a doubt he could have made better, when someone plopped onto the seat next to him. He took another bite, fighting the urge to roll his eyes in annoyance. There were plenty of other seats available.

The heat of a stare warmed his cheek, and he glanced over, an eyebrow raised. Bright hazel eyes met his, set in a face completely covered in freckles, cheeks stretched with a friendly smile.

Campbell returned his attention to his food. "Didn't your mother ever tell you it's rude to stare?"

"She died before she could tell me anything at all." The girl's tone was as cheerful as the glint in her eyes.

Campbell set the sandwich on a plate, turning to face her. "My condolences. Let me officially inform you, then: it's rude to stare."

"You're heading west?" she asked without pause.

Campbell narrowed his eyes, distrust shining from indigo depths. Like him, the female was young, but he knew better than to assume that meant she wasn't dangerous.

"I overheard you asking for directions earlier," she said dismissively. "You have a job on the coast?"

"It's rude to eavesdrop, too," he answered.

"I'm heading out to West Eyko as well, but making a short stop first in Umbra. We could be road buddies."

Campbell truly looked at her, then. Mischief flashed through her eyes, and his suspicions doubled.

"I'm Aleah." She stuck out her hand, tucking a lock of straight red hair behind a clipped ear.

"I travel alone." He turned back to his plate, but all of his senses were tuned to her, ready to react if she tried anything.

Aleah only frowned, dropping her hand. "Look, I won't lie, I've been following you for a couple days, and—"

"You've been *following* me?" He whipped around to face her, barely restraining himself from palming the knife at his hip. Unease crawled up his spine as he tried to recall any indication of being watched.

Aleah held her hands up. "Not in a creepy way! I just happened to see you lurking around the overseer's establishment and just sort of ... camped out to watch what would happen. You've got major talent."

"You watched me?" Campbell's heart rate doubled, wondering how he'd been so careless not to notice.

"Well, yeah, I thought for a moment we had the same target, but turns out that was just a misunderstanding and—"

"Wait, what are you on about?"

Aleah tipped her head to the side, confusion clouding her face. "The crystal dagger. That was—"

Campbell leaned forward, slapping his palm over Aleah's mouth. He looked around, but the few other patrons of the bar were tucked away into their own corners, no one acknowledging them.

Aleah forced her tongue between her lips, swiping it across the faintly salty skin of his palm.

He yelped, pulling his hand back and wiping it on the leg of his pants.

She glared, folding her arms across her chest. "Next time I'll bite," she promised. "Now, would you quit interrupting me? Legends."

"How do you know about the dagger?" Campbell asked, his voice low. Caution and curiosity warred in his chest. No one should have known the dagger was missing until he was well out of town.

Aleah rolled her eyes. "Actually, I take it back. You're a little slower than I anticipated." She slid from her stool, heading for the door.

"Slow?" Campbell questioned, following her. Part of him wilted at leaving the food behind, but he consoled himself with the knowledge that it wasn't anything great. More importantly, he needed to know more about this wraith who'd shadowed him for days without notice.

Aleah pushed the door open, turning her head to give him a look that screamed *you're proving my point* before stepping out into the street, Campbell only a few steps behind.

The streets glistened in the lamplight as rain fell from the sky. Aleah again turned to look at him, flashing a sly grin before taking off down the street. Her feet seemed to find every puddle along the road, and laughter echoed from her as water splashed up around her boots.

Campbell stared dumbly after her, rain weighing down his curls and dripping from his antlers. There had been a definite challenge in her eyes, and he was surprised that it didn't scare him so much as intrigue him. He took off after her, long, powerful strides quickly eating up the distance between them. She put on an extra burst of speed when he neared, but he easily kept pace until she slowed, laughing as she caught her breath.

"How did you know I took the dagger?" he asked, lacking the bite he'd intended. Her jubilant demeanor was infectious, and intuition told him that if she'd meant him harm, she'd have done it already.

Aleah smiled, raindrops clinging to her lashes. "I told you, I saw you, and I was curious. So I waited. Watched. And again, I say, well done. If I could be even half as quick-handed a thief, Sekha would have another thing coming."

Though he was still confused, Campbell's lips twitched at the compliment, and his posture relaxed slightly. "I staked out the estate for two days and never once saw you."

Aleah's grin widened. "I'm a clumsy thief, but I excel in surveillance, among other things."

Despite the concern that still turned heavy in his stomach, Campbell felt himself warming to her, and that only confused him more. "You're a mercenary?"

She bowed with a flourish.

"Are you always so friendly and open with other outlaws?" Even when he'd worked as part of a group, he'd never felt the kind of easy camaraderie she exuded.

"I'm a good judge of character."

Campbell huffed out a laugh as he shivered, rainwater soaking his clothes and making the fabric stick to his skin. He clenched his teeth together to keep them from chattering as he studied her, contemplating whether or not to give in to that sudden yearning for companionship. "You said you're heading west?"

Aleah nodded.

"Campbell." He stuck out his hand, curiosity winning out over caution.

Aleah shook it, that mischievous light coming back to her eyes. "Meet me in the square in the morning. We'll grab breakfast on the way out."

Campbell agreed, and she turned, skipping off toward the inn she'd booked for the night. He watched her disappear before heading back to his own accommodations. He couldn't shake the feeling that something important had just happened, which unsettled him more than the fact that he'd been watched. As he stripped down to shower, he did his best to ignore it. Campbell worked alone.

He'd been with a band of mercenaries before. They'd picked him up when he was young, taught him how to be quick with his fingers. But they'd also taught him other lessons.

Mainly, that no one could be trusted: no one had anyone's best interest in mind other than their own. Every single one of them would rat the others out without hesitation to save their own skin. They were all depraved and took advantage of each other often. The people he'd been with were often bruised and bloodied, fighting to hold their place on the higher rungs of the group.

But even with the infighting, it was safer than being on the streets, safer than being alone. Campbell had held his own for a while, thinking there was no other place for him in the world, until one of the other males had attacked him at night.

Hot water streamed down Campbell's back, and he relished the burn as memories of the encounter flashed through his mind. He'd been asleep when the male had crawled onto his cot, pressing his front to Campbell's back, slipping a hand into his pants, gripping him so firmly that Campbell had been scared to move.

"Just relax." Hot breath had fluttered across Campbell's cheek, and his hand slid beneath his pillow, gripping the hilt of the knife he kept there.

He'd recognized the voice, and his stomach fluttered with unease. The male behind him was high fae, which had always made Campbell nervous when around him. Because of the vast amount of opportunities presented to them, it was extremely unusual for a high fae, a magic-wielding person, to lead any sort of outwardly unlawful life. That alone had told Campbell this male was dangerous, and he'd always kept his distance.

The fae had moved his hands, working to slide Campbell's pants down, continuing to whisper reassurances in his ear, and with one deep breath in, Campbell pulled the knife from under his head and swung his arm back behind him.

The blade had ended up buried in the male's bicep, and he'd cursed loudly as Campbell rolled away from him, springing to his feet and launching toward the door. He leapt over sleeping bodies, some roused by the noise, and bolted at a dead sprint.

He was fast, faster than any of the others in his guild, and that singular bit of knowledge kept his stride smooth and confident as he ran from the building that had been his home, as he ran from everything he knew, heart pounding in his chest.

Life alone was difficult, but relying on others to keep him safe wasn't an option.

In the two days it took them to reach Umbra, Campbell decided he very much enjoyed Aleah's company. Their banter was quick and easy, and it was almost unsettling how comfortable he was around her, poking fun and being teased in return. He couldn't remember the last time he'd so thoroughly enjoyed someone's company.

Aleah was currently describing the training room she'd helped build, her hands waving and voice bright with excitement. Campbell knew she was trying to tempt him to stay and had told her multiple times that he had no interest in joining their group. But that didn't mean he couldn't have a friend, right?

Even if the prospect of friendship was a pleasant one, he still wasn't sure how he felt about staying the night in Umbra. "You really live here, right under the Crown's nose?"

Aleah shrugged, leading him down the street with a posture that suggested complete ease. "Jasper knows the heir apparent, and Mer is the younger prince's best friend, so we have a sort of deal worked out with the Crown. We're left alone, and whenever they need something unsavory done, we help out. Add in Umbra's central location in Sekha, and it only makes sense to operate from here."

Campbell frowned, but nodded. The thought of being in a house with all of those people made his stomach turn with anxiety, but Aleah had assured him he'd have his own room, and she was also fairly certain that not everyone would be home.

Home.

It was a strange word to him. One he hadn't claimed in longer than he cared to think about.

Aleah grabbed his hand, pulling him into an alley as she slipped a key from a small pouch on her belt. She led him through a dim hallway that opened up into a common room lit by overhead lighting. Two couches took up the back wall and one side, a low table between them. "This is the mushroom, it's where we hang out." Aleah waved her hand toward the area, walking over to a door in the wall next to them and peering inside. No light shone from the room, and she sighed, moving behind Campbell to the staircase next to him. "Hang tight, the others might be upstairs."

Campbell watched her bound up the stairs, then jumped when he turned his head to meet the fierce gaze of a falcon perched in the entryway of the kitchen. His eyes flicked from the bird to the stove and counter space, not sure which was more enticing.

"Hello, friend," he finally said, tucking his hands into his pockets to keep from reaching out to pet the predator. "I don't think Aleah mentioned you, which feels like a crime." The falcon tipped his head to the side, clicking his beak a couple times and watching as Campbell walked past and into the kitchen, awe sparkling in his indigo eyes as he took it all in. He turned back to look at the bird with a conspiratorial smile. "This kitchen is almost as beautiful as you."

Panic was familiar with that word, and fluffed out his chest, tilting his head up in approval at the praise.

A knife block next to the sink caught Campbell's eye, and he couldn't help himself. He slid out a few of the knives, pulling a chef's knife all the way free and holding it up to examine the blade.

A small chirrup interrupted him, and he turned his head to find the falcon watching him intently.

"Sorry, buddy, I don't have any food. But I could make you *such* a pretty pâté with this collection." Campbell turned back to the knives with a mournful sigh, returning the chef's blade to pull out a paring knife, the tip curved up to a beautiful point.

"Are you dirty-talking my bird?"

Campbell jumped at the voice, instinctively twisting the knife in his fingers, pressing the flat of the blade against his forearm as he looked toward the base of the stairs. "Maybe," he answered, meeting a wary blue gaze. His irritation at having been caught so completely off guard became something closer to mortification when he took in the man now blocking his exit.

He was leaning against the wall like the building might topple over without his support. His torso was bare, arms covered in colorful tattoos of birds, and his pants hung low on his hips, one leg crossed casually over the other. The ends of his short blonde hair were combed up in the front, and those cold blue eyes trailed down Campbell's body and back up to the tops of his antlers before settling again on his face.

Campbell felt his cheeks heat at the unabashed appraisal, even if he had just done the same, and he folded his arms across his chest, careful of the hidden knife, raising his chin in defiance.

A smirk pulled at one edge of the man's mouth as the bird hopped from the perch onto one broad shoulder.

"Leo, you giant troll, get out of the way," Aleah huffed, pushing past him.

Leonidas barely shifted as Aleah brushed by, his eyes still on Campbell. "Another stray, Aleah?"

Campbell narrowed his eyes defensively, but Aleah spoke before he had a chance to retort.

"He's a thief, and better than any I've ever seen." Aleah hopped onto the counter at the back of the kitchen, swinging her feet in front of her. "*And* he can cook."

Leonidas' gaze drifted to Aleah, one golden eyebrow raised skeptically.

"He took the crystal dagger. *The* crystal dagger."

Leonidas looked back at Campbell, his posture remaining casual but his expression betraying his fascination. "Did you?"

With a casual shrug, Campbell let his arms fall, dropping the knife hilt-first into his pocket in the same motion.

"Show him!" Aleah pressed, excitement in her voice.

Her enthusiasm was both contagious and incredibly inflating to his ego, and Campbell had to bite the inside of his cheek to keep from grinning as he slid his pack from his shoulders, pulling out a wad of cloth. Dropping the pack to the floor, he unwrapped the cloth, revealing a dagger carved entirely from crystal, the facets of the blade catching the light and sending prisms dancing across the wall. It was one of the most famous pieces of art in all of Nethyl, said to be carved by the Legend Serafine in the days before the first Keeper, when monsters slipped from other realms from time to time through the unguarded Gate and wreaked havoc on the world.

"Legends be damned." Leonidas nodded his head appreciatively. "How'd you manage that?"

Campbell wrapped the dagger back up, returning it to his bag. This time, he couldn't hold back the smile that pulled at his lips. "I'm the best."

Something curled through Leonidas' stomach at the simple answer. He could appreciate the steady confidence that came with excelling in an area not many had mastered. And *fuck* if it wasn't attractive.

"Like I was telling you, he's going to go to West Eyko with us. That's where his client is."

Campbell looked over his shoulder at her, his smile evaporating with his surprise. "I'm not going with *you*. You asked to tag along with *me*. And I don't remember agreeing to additional party members." *Even if they are exceptionally nice to look at.*

"Yeah, yeah, you travel alone." Aleah rolled her eyes. "But you've been traveling with me, haven't you? And I'm way more dangerous than Leo."

Leonidas frowned. "She's not wrong. That girl has a higher body count than the rest of us combined."

"Like that's even saying anything when you, Mer, and Calysta can count your death tolls on a single hand." Aleah waved off the statement.

Campbell clicked his tongue, inadvertently drawing Panic's attention as he shouldered his bag. "Great. I've booked myself a room in a den of murderers," he muttered, shaking his head. "Look, I appreciate the offer, but I really am not a group activities sort of person. I should go." He gave Aleah a grim smile, then stepped toward Leonidas. "Beautiful falcon," he complimented, waiting for the tall, muscular blonde to step out of his way.

Leonidas turned his body, forcing Campbell to squeeze past him. He gave himself a moment to admire the taut muscles of the male's ass, clearly conditioned from years of running, before he spoke. "Hey, buck."

Campbell paused, unprepared for the warmth that spread through him at the nickname and the tone with which it was delivered.

"If you're going to take that knife I spent so much time honing, I think it's only fair you use it to make me dinner first."

Campbell pressed his lips together, turning back around and giving the man a thorough once-over. "Well, in the name of fairness."

"Aleah said you're a decent cook?" Leonidas prompted.

"She lied." Campbell lifted his chin, meeting Leonidas' gaze. "I'm an *excellent* cook."

Leonidas raised an eyebrow.

"You're impressed that I stole the dagger?" Campbell asked sweetly, tipping his head to the side as he pulled the pilfered knife from his pocket. "My true talents lie in food."

A smirk twitched on the man's lips, and he held out an arm in invitation toward the kitchen. "Prove yourself then."

Campbell told himself he was only making the most of what was available to him and not purposefully showing off as he cooked. Venison steaks were prepared with shaved garlic and seared with butter, sweet onions, and thyme and accompanied by a medley of roasted vegetables sprinkled with garlic salt and shredded cheese.

While they ate, Aleah convinced him to share the story of how he managed to steal one of the most guarded weapons in Sekha, and Leonidas found himself impressed, both with the food and the male's quick fingers. He begrudgingly admitted he'd only known about the paring knife because he saw the missing slot in the knife block when Campbell left.

Jasper and Calysta arrived in the middle of the meal, but the unease Campbell expected to feel with being around so many mercenaries again never fully surfaced. The dynamics in this group were worlds different than those of the guild he'd previously been a part of, and before he fell asleep that night in his promised room, he agreed to traveling with Aleah and Leonidas on their way to West Eyko.

Leonidas intrigued him. Though he clearly had a soft spot for Panic and his other birds, the man had a tough exterior, and his attitude toward anything job-related was completely no-nonsense.

Aleah, on the other hand, found a way to turn anything and everything into a joke, and was almost vibrating with energy at all times.

Campbell played off of everything Aleah did, and he found pleasure in the way it clearly irritated Leonidas. He'd been nervous at first, but the glint in Leonidas' eyes almost challenged Campbell to push him, and when he broke, he was the furthest thing from the violence that Campbell had expected.

It took a lot, but between the two of them, Aleah and Campbell wore Leonidas down until he would share in the jokes, and when he did drop that gruff exterior, the innuendos in his comments heated Campbell from the inside out, turning knots in his belly and making his toes curl as he suppressed the urge to push further.

That journey through western Sekha's giant mountains took five days by horse. They reached a split in the main road in West Eyko, where Campbell would be heading north and the others continuing to the coast.

"Where are you going after this?" Aleah asked, her horse shifting restlessly beneath her.

Campbell shrugged. "Wherever the jobs are."

"Well," Aleah started slowly, eyes darting to Leonidas. "We'll be back this way in four days. We can meet up here if you want to go back into Umbra. Leo gets a lot of leads for different jobs at the aviary. There could be something worthwhile, if you don't have anything else already lined up."

Campbell looked at Leonidas, who was busy readjusting his reins. "I'll think about it." He knew if he went back with them, Aleah would try to convince him to join their troupe, and the thought of depending on others filled him with anxiety. But he'd be lying if he said he hadn't enjoyed her company and how much fun it was to band with her to tease Leonidas.

A different kind of nerves fluttered to life in his gut with the memory of some of those flirtatious remarks, and he barely kept himself from looking back at the man.

"We'll camp here that fourth night. Join us if you'd like," Aleah said before waving goodbye and turning her horse away.

Leonidas pulled up next to Campbell. "I'll see you around, buck."

Campbell watched the two continue through the forest before turning his own horse north. Maybe there wouldn't be any harm in meeting back up with them. At the very least, he could wind up with another job. He told himself that was the only reason he was considering it, that it had nothing to do with the thought of Leonidas on his knees in front of him, lips wrapped around his cock. Or what it would feel like to be pressed against a wall, Leonidas pushing inside of him.

Campbell adjusted himself in his pants, angrily pushing the visuals away. "Think with the head on your shoulders, dumbass."

Chapter 9

I need a favor

Leonidas woke up sweating. At some point in the night, Campbell had thrown his half of the blankets on top of him, and was now sleeping peacefully on his stomach, one arm draped over the side of the bed. Rolling to face him, Leonidas lifted a hand to run his fingers into soft, dark curls. The adjustment period when they'd first started sharing a bed had been rough, to say the least. Every night that first week, multiple times a night, Leonidas had been woken by the point of an antler sticking into his cheek or his neck or his temple. They'd eventually figured it out, and even though they only rarely stayed pressed against each other through the night, being able to simply reach out and touch Campbell at any time had given Leonidas some of the best sleep of his life.

He pressed a kiss to the base of Campbell's neck, his pale fingers sliding down the tan skin of the male's back before he stood.

Panic was sleeping on a pedestal across the room, head tucked against his back. Leonidas stroked a finger down the bird's chest to wake him, and Panic's head rolled up, blinking sleepily at Leonidas before stepping up onto his hand.

He walked down the hall into the office, opening the window there.

Panic jumped down to the ledge, peering up indignantly.

Leonidas cocked an eyebrow and gestured outside. "Nope. If you want breakfast, go find it."

Panic ruffled his feathers.

Leonidas made a clicking noise from the side of his mouth, holding up a hand and setting the other on top of it, a command for the falcon to return when the sun was fully over the mountains. "I've got places to be today. Don't be late," he said as Panic flew off.

He ran drills in the training room, sweat dripping from his skin by the time he finished. After showering, he found Campbell in the kitchen making breakfast.

When Leonidas walked in, Campbell's eyes traveled unabashedly over every inch of exposed skin. The colorful tattoos on the man's arms had been there for years, but the tattoo on his chest was newer: a pair of antlers with a Bonding rune in the middle, centered over his sternum. The ink had been mixed with Campbell's blood, bestowing Leonidas with a little bit of the magic that he possessed. Now his healing was slightly accelerated, his immune system stronger, and, most importantly, his lifespan would extend far past that of a normal human.

Campbell turned back to the stove, pushing bacon around in a pan. "Quit being so pretty. It's rude."

Leonidas watched him for a moment, something in his chest expanding at the comfortable normalcy of the scene. How many times had he walked into the kitchen to Campbell cooking? How many times had he brushed a kiss against his lips, made a flirtatious comment, and gone about his day? Four years of routine, four years of loving that male, and it suddenly struck him that they were alone. They didn't have to share the space, share their time, and a possessive, hungry lust rolled through him, his cock twitching in his pants.

"I never claimed to be polite." Leonidas walked up behind him, hooking a finger over a prong of his antlers to tip his head to the side and feather kisses along his jaw.

That tug against Campbell's skull went straight down his spine, pooling low in his abdomen. "Let me move the bacon out and I'll start on some eggs," he said, pretending like his pants weren't growing uncomfortably tight as Leonidas moved slowly down his neck.

"I think I'd rather sausage," Leonidas murmured against his neck.

Campbell laughed, turning off the burner. "Legends, Leonidas, that's the most corny—oh, fuck." His laughter cut off when Leonidas grabbed his hips and spun him around, pushing him against the counter. He rose onto his toes, snaking his arms around Leonidas' neck and pulling him into a kiss.

Leonidas lifted a hand to Campbell's neck, thumb brushing his jaw and tongue sweeping into his mouth, hungry and wanting.

With a groan, Campbell dropped his hands down to grip the waist of Leonidas's pants, tugging him closer and easing a hand between their bodies to drag down the length of Leonidas' cock.

Leonidas pushed back, grinding against Campbell's touch as he slid one hand up into his hair and around the base of an antler. Tilting the fae's head to the side, he drew the flat of his tongue up the expanse of skin now exposed to him.

"Leo," Campbell panted needily, desire coiled hot in his belly and his cock throbbing against his laces.

Leonidas dropped to his knees, kissing Campbell's abdomen just above the waistline of his pants. "Your skin is so fucking soft, do you know that?" he whispered, his thumbs drawing circles over Campbell's hips as he moved his mouth across his belly.

Campbell gasped, one hand gripping the edge of the counter as the other slid through the man's short blonde hair. "Leo, please."

"You beg so pretty, Cam," he hummed with approval, deftly untying the laces of Campbell's pants and pulling them down. He wrapped the fingers of one hand around the hardened length in front of him, stroking from tip to base. "Tell me what you want."

Campbell's hips bucked against Leo's grasp, his head falling back. "I want—" His breathing hitched as Leonidas stroked him, running his thumb over the tip of his cock, catching the bead of pre-come there and spreading it. "I want your mouth, Leo. I want your mouth and then I want your c—" his words turned into a low moan as Leonidas took him, lips a tight warmth and tongue gliding over skin as he sucked.

Leonidas groaned around him, bobbing his head as his hands ran possessively over the muscle of Campbell's legs and ass.

"Oh, *fuck.*" Campbell flexed his hips, his fingers splaying over the back of Leonidas' head and his own falling back as he thrust further down Leonidas' throat.

Leonidas was straining against his own pants, cock painfully hard as he looked up, watching Campbell lose himself to ecstasy. Ecstasy *he* was responsible for causing. Pulling the cock from his mouth, Leonidas slowly pumped it with a fist as he met Campbell's indigo eyes, lit wildly with lust. "You're eager this morning, buck." He brought a finger to his mouth, keeping eye contact as he sucked on it, and the digit glistened as he drew it back.

"*Me?*" Campbell gasped, still thrusting against Leonidas's grip. But any argument he wanted to make died on his lips as Leonidas dropped his mouth back over his cock. He felt the cool wetness of the finger press against his asshole, and an undignified whimper crawled up his throat. "Please, Leo," he begged, rocking his hips.

One of Leonidas's hands still tightly gripped Campbell's thigh as the fae thrust deep into his mouth. He pushed his finger into Campbell, and another plea fell from his lips, hitched into a whine. Hearing Campbell beg for him was almost enough to make Leonidas come in his pants, it was so Legends-damned *pretty.* A dribble of come spilled onto his tongue, and he swallowed around Campbell with a groan of approval.

Campbell panted, both of his hands now gripping Leonidas' head as heat rippled up his spine, his heels pushing against the floor and toes curling. Leonidas kept working that finger inside him, and pressure built from low in his gut, his heart thundering against his chest and mouth dropping open in a heavy, whimpering gasp as his orgasm tore through him.

Swallowing the come that filled his mouth, Leonidas let Campbell drop down slowly from the edge before slipping his finger free. He pulled Campbell's pants up as he stood, tugging him into a deep kiss as he retied the laces.

Campbell could taste himself on Leonidas' tongue, and he reached down between them, Leonidas still hard as a rock.

Breaking the kiss, Leonidas brushed his thumb over Campbell's bottom lip, a self-satisfied smirk pulling at his mouth. Then he stepped away, washing his hands before grabbing a loaf of bread and a knife. "I'll be at the castle for the majority of the day. Horscha should be aware already, but if you don't mind, would you stop by with some food for her if you get a chance?"

Campbell blinked, still catching his breath. "What?"

"Do you mind dropping by the aviary with some food for Horscha at some point today?" Leonidas repeated, cutting a few slices of bread.

Campbell swallowed, turning back to the stove and moving bacon from the pan as his cheeks flushed. "Oh, yeah, of course." The cast iron had held the heat well, and he cracked a couple of eggs into it, trying to act like his legs weren't still jelly.

"If I didn't have a schedule to keep, I'd take that tight little ass right now," Leonidas murmured, stepping behind Campbell and wrapping his arms around his waist. "But I can wait until tonight." He stole a strip of bacon before moving away again.

A delicious shiver ran down Campbell's spine, and he looked over his shoulder, watching Leonidas pull down plates and cups. "So incredibly rude," he reiterated the earlier sentiment, and Leonidas only winked at him.

After breakfast, Leonidas went back upstairs to don a shirt and close the office window. Panic was sitting on the roof of the aviary across the alley and swooped inside when he saw the human.

"Felt good to get out and stretch your wings, didn't it?" Leonidas scratched his head, letting the falcon settle on his shoulder.

The late summer air was cool, right on the cusp of tipping into fall, and Leonidas breathed it in gratefully as he walked to the castle. He hated summer. The sun burned his fair skin, its brightness was harsh against his light eyes, and the heat made him irritable. He was ready for the cooler months and the heavier cloud cover and foggier mornings that typically accompanied them.

Leonidas usually spent one day every few weeks up at the castle, sometimes exchanging birds that had come from one place or another delivering messages, sometimes just to help train new falcons or people new to working in the aviary. He'd fostered good friendships with all the long-term attendants, and his natural knack for communicating with the birds had grown him a considerable reputation.

He opened the outer door to the aviary and almost collided with Mollian, sending Panic up into the air with a disgruntled screech.

"Leo! It's good to see you."

"I've missed having you around," Leonidas replied sincerely as Panic lighted back on his shoulder, peering down at the king before tilting his head around.

"She's not here, bud," Mollian addressed the bird.

Panic, having come to the same conclusion, clicked his beak at the audacity.

"We should plan something when they're back in town," Leonidas suggested. "I know Aleah will want an excuse to cut loose, and Mer will need a break from all the politics."

Mollian laughed, brushing a curl from his forehead. "I'm lucky she loves me, because Legends know I would throw myself into the harbor if I had to run that interference. I'll keep my schedule clear." The king paused for a moment, shoving his hands into his pockets as a line of worry creased his brow. Then he tilted his head, gesturing for Leonidas to follow him as he moved away from the aviary. "I need a favor," he said when they were out of earshot of anyone exiting the building.

"Anything," Leonidas answered, taken aback by how fully he meant it.

"Is there a way that you can find an excuse to be here more often? I need you to keep an eye on any correspondence coming in for Ferrick, even just to know who he's talking to and how often they're sending messages."

Leonidas' eyebrows twitched only the slightest amount in surprise. "Is there anything you're looking for that I should keep a closer watch on? Birds going to or coming from a specific area?"

Mollian blew out a slow breath, running a hand through his hair, and Leonidas was struck with the realization of how alone he must feel in his own court. He had friends and advisors, but almost all of them were people who expected him to be a king and to know what he was doing. There were not many people he could just be Mollian around, and that had to be exhausting. "I don't even know," he answered. He cast a furtive glance over his shoulder. "Bellamy saw one of the other Rangers watching Ryddan. Spying on him from the trees, and ..." he shook his head.

Leonidas bristled, crossing his arms over his chest. "Leave it to that piece of shit to feel threatened by a child."

Mollian nodded, his shoulders relaxing as relief flooded him. Knowing there was help outside of Bellamy, people he could trust, lifted a heavy weight from his chest. "I just need him to give me an irrefutable reason to exile him, but I don't want anyone getting hurt in the process."

"I'll keep an eye on his correspondence," Leonidas assured him. "And tell Bellamy to bring the little prince by sometime soon."

"I'll pass it along," Mollian promised.

Leonidas moved into the aviary, Panic standing tall on his shoulder as they passed the various caged birds, knowing he was more important than any of them. The workday was light, and Leonidas easily lost himself in exercising the hawks and falcons, keeping their commands fresh in their minds. Just before he left, a couple of young guardsmen came in to clean cages and perches, and Leonidas caught the eye of the head keeper on duty. "Are they just on rotation or trying to become falconers?"

"They're falconer hopefuls," she answered, arching an eyebrow. "I don't suppose you want to test their mettle? Show them a couple tricks?"

"I've got a pretty light couple of weeks, actually, so I might just be able to. Let me double check that Horscha will be available to watch things," he answered smoothly.

"Wait, really?" The keeper beamed at him. "Don't tell the coinmaster I said it, but we really should be paying you more. Hey Seb, Torra, come over here," she called to the younger guardsmen. "You need to meet Leo; he's an absolute Legend with birds like you wouldn't even believe."

Leonidas barely held back his smile, the excuse to hang around and keep an eye on things coming easier than if he'd planned it. He straightened his shoulders, turning to meet the fae that approached him with wide, eager eyes. Their gazes focused on Panic, who matched Leonidas' smooth energy, eager for the fawning he knew was coming, but too prideful to preen for it in front of these young strangers.

Chapter 10

Rules to follow

ALEAH AND JASPER BOOKED a room at a small establishment on the outskirts of Do Lech. It was close enough to Red Marsh for easy travel and surveillance on Illiziana, and Jasper was able to scope everything out for Merriam while also keeping an eye on Aleah, able to assess her body language and moods and step in if she started to fall into a full spiral. Though she would never admit it, Aleah slept easier, knowing Jasper was in the other bed.

The first night there, they slept with the window open, and the scent of the sea breeze had woven into Aleah's dreams. She'd been just on the cusp of six, not yet tormented enough to have learned to hide herself, and had run through the halls of the estate with her arms full of shells she'd found on the beach. She'd run straight into Chetney, and he'd carved her belly with the sharp edge of one of those shells for the inconvenience.

She woke up from the memory-dream in a cold sweat, shutting the window and sinking to the floor below, arms wrapped around her knees as she stared into the dark.

As much as she assured herself that her family didn't know she was here—Hel, probably didn't even know she was alive—she couldn't shake the irrational fear that she would wake up in the night with Chetney looming over her, lips curled in a hateful sneer as he prepared to rip her from her bed and catch up on years of torment, years of teaching her that she should never have been born.

But Aleah didn't give herself a chance to focus on any of that. She threw herself into her work, learning everything she could about Illiziana Fielder and her routine.

Red Marsh was a few klicks further down the bay than Do Lech, but it wasn't too long of a trek. Aleah alternated her forms of travel to avoid recognition and suspicion, sometimes traveling by ferry, sometimes taking a horse, and sometimes walking or tagging along on a cart going to trade goods from one town to the other.

Aleah's first day in Red Marsh was spent walking around town, listening in on idle conversation or casually broaching the subject of the overseer with shop owners and fishermen.

Opinions were mostly neutral, but it became very clear, very quickly, that Illiziana was not well-loved by nymphs. Decades ago, she had set in place regulations about where and when they could hold ceremonies and in what numbers they could gather. Some thought the regulations were smart—who knew what could come of that level of blood magic being unleashed at will—while others thought it was unsavory to try to control the practices of fair folk, regardless of what magic they may or may not possess.

"It's best not to anger the water nymphs when you run a fishing town, that's all I've got to say on the matter," the captain of a small fishing vessel had told her.

"We all have rules to follow, blood magic or no, that's part of living in a society!" a barmaid had insisted.

One nymph pulled Aleah aside and told her that Illiziana had even gone so far as to suggest nymphs be made to wear iron to put a damper on their magic while in town. "She wants to make slaves of us, I bet. What other reason is there for her obsession with us and our magic?"

Whether or not this was true, the very thought made Aleah's stomach turn.

Regardless of what the overseer stood for or how her people felt about her, Aleah was not there to play judge, only executioner.

She watched the overseer's estate closely, changing vantage points every few hours and staying hidden through years of practice as she gauged any weak points in security that might make her job easier, learning the guard rotation and patrol schedule and what sort of armory they appeared to have.

One day, Illiziana left by carriage, and Aleah overheard one of her attendants say something about a trip to Do Lech. It was the perfect opportunity to break into the estate and learn the layout of the inside. Slipping through an upstairs window by way of a tall willow growing nearby, Aleah looked around, opening a closet and grabbing a stack of towels. If anyone saw her, she could just pretend to be a new hire tidying up. If that was unbelievable, a towel over the head could buy her enough time to disappear.

Aleah crept through the expansive home, but it seemed mostly devoid of staff. She'd heard people a few times, but had always been able to dip into a room or hide behind furniture to avoid being seen. She kept her foray short and sweet before heading back to the inn to sketch out a plan.

Calysta was sitting on her bed when she returned, a basket of berries beside her.

"Hey, stranger." Aleah smiled, plopping down next to the nymph. Calysta had parted ways with Jasper and Aleah once they'd arrived at the inn, heading off to do what Aleah affectionately called "her nymphy thing."

Taking a handful of berries, Calysta relaxed further against the head-board, popping them into her mouth one at a time. "Have I ever told you how much better company you guys make than my own kind?"

"Once or twice." Aleah leaned over to grab writing materials from the bedside table. "Want to help me plan?"

"Absolutely."

"Hey, you're from around here, too, aren't you?"

Calysta waved a hand noncommittally. "The general south, mostly."

"Do you know much about the overseer of Red Marsh?"

"Illiziana? I know she fought her way tooth and nail to power and got in close with Spiro Kinbriar. And I know she's never been a friend to nymphs, regardless of what she may tell herself or other people." Calysta speared a berry with one claw-tipped finger. "Is she your target?" Her pitch-black eyes remained fixed on the fruit.

Aleah nodded, tucking her hair behind her ear and beginning her sketch of the estate.

Calysta's eyebrows shot up. "Wow. I hope you asked a pretty price for her head."

Aleah gave her a look from the corner of her eye, snatching up some berries. "Not only am I a professional, Calysta, but I'm also the best of the best. I absolutely charged what I'm worth for a job of this capacity."

If Calysta didn't know her any better, she might be disturbed at the easy smile on the half-fae's face as she talked so flippantly about murder. But not only did she know Aleah, she also understood the necessity of being able to separate herself from jobs. "What've you got?" She pulled her long, pink hair over one shoulder, leaning forward to peer at the sketch Aleah had drawn.

"From what I can tell, she usually sleeps alone, so that'll be the quickest and quietest bet. I can be in and out and back here before anyone even realizes she's not going to wake up." Aleah finished her sketch of the house, holding it out for Calysta to see where she'd marked typical guard routes, entry points, and possible obstacles.

"Let's run through the plan, then."

Aleah talked it through, Calysta offering suggestions or pointing out potential problems throughout. They'd just about wrapped it up when Jasper came in.

"Up to no good?" Aleah asked, drawing a new picture over her map of the overseer's house.

"The usual," Jasper answered, lowering onto his bed. "How are you doing?"

Aleah began ripping the paper into tiny pieces. "I've got a plan. Now just to set everything in motion. Have you seen Mer recently?"

Jasper shook his head. "She's been kept on a pretty tight schedule during the day, but she did send a message saying she'd try to make it out one of these nights."

"I hope she's doing okay. I hate to think of her locked away in that compound with no friends." Aleah's shoulders hunched, but before she had a chance to sink into the depths of her old fears, a knock sounded at the door.

"I heard this is where the party's at," Kodi announced as Jasper let him in.

Aleah choked back a squeal, jumping from the bed to throw her arms around the Ranger. She shouldn't have been caught off guard by how much the sight of him affected her, but her chest tightened, her breath catching in her throat and the sting of tears in her eyes.

"I'm sorry I couldn't slip away sooner," he whispered into her hair.

Afraid her voice would crack if she spoke, Aleah bit his shoulder, tightening her arms around him while she composed herself.

"Have any of you eaten yet?" Jasper asked as Aleah dropped back to her feet. "I was about to have food sent up."

Aleah looked at Kodi. "Stay for supper?"

"You have me for the night, little merc."

She let the term of endearment warm her through the middle and snuggled into his side. Part of her reasoned that some night recon might be helpful, but she pushed thoughts of the job aside, content to let her world exist only in that room in the inn, surrounded by people who made her feel safe and happy.

Chapter 11

Sweet girl

ALEAH HIKED INTO RED Marsh after dusk the next evening. She sat on a hill outside of the estate, cloak wrapped around her and hood over her head as she stared through the dense brush.

Unwanted thoughts kept running around her mind.

She knows our grandfather.

Did she know our mother?

Would she know us?

Did she know us?

Aleah was struck with the sudden realization that *she* should know Illiziana. Even if the overseer was busy running her own town, with the amount of events the Kinbriars held, it wouldn't be unthinkable for Illiziana to have been around several times a year.

Clutching her cloak more tightly around herself, Aleah rested her chin on her knees, concentrating on the main gate of the estate as she dug through memories.

She could remember being very young, surrounded by her family and feeling safe and excited as their home was filled with strange people, but none of them had faces. A frown creased her brow as she tried to recall celebrations from when she'd been older.

She could remember her nursemaid helping her dress and styling her hair, always pinning it to where it would fall over her clipped ear. She could remember her belly churning with nerves as she stressed about whether or not anyone else would bring their children, and what games they would want to play. And even if there were no other children present, what questions would the grown-ups ask her? What would they want to joke about or pretend to confide in her, winking as they asked her to keep a secret about slipping her an extra dessert or something else that should be innocent and fun?

But her uncle was incredibly suspicious and didn't trust her talking to anyone else. Every act of kindness was a possible bribe, trying to pull secrets from her. Secrets that her grandparents stressed she must never, never tell anyone.

"You must try harder to stay out of his way, sweet girl," Larna would tell her, dabbing lightly at a gash along her side with antiseptic before bandaging it up. "You know he sometimes has a temper."

Aleah would nod, holding her lower lip in her mouth to keep it from trembling, swallowing down tears and forcing even breaths through her nose.

"We love you, and so does your uncle. He's just hurting," Larna would remind her, smoothing her hair back, but never tucking it behind her clipped ear.

"You must never tell anyone about this, Aleah, no matter what," Spiro would say, sliding a plate of caramel-drizzled apples across the counter as she sucked in small, shallow breaths to alleviate the pain in her ribs. "It's not him, you understand. Something else comes over him and takes control, but he's working on it. He's trying to get better."

Aleah would nod numbly, reaching out for the offered sweet.

Spiro would pull the plate back, just slightly out of reach. "He's family, Aleah. That means more than anything else. He's family, and we have to help him get better, but we can't do that if you tell. You understand, don't you? Family first? No matter what?"

Aleah would meet Spiro's earnest, pleading gaze with hazel eyes devoid of emotion. "Family first. No matter what," she would whisper, and the treat would be pushed back into her reach.

"That's our sweet girl. We love you."

Aleah took a deep, shuddering breath, biting her cheek hard to force back the long-buried memories of her grandparents. "Parties," she reminded herself. "Think about the parties."

But no memories of the parties themselves or specifics about the attendees would surface. All she could recall was keeping tabs on where Chetney was, if he was watching her, if he was close.

A surge of panic clawed up Aleah's chest, tremors shaking her from the inside out. She wrapped her hand around a bramble and squeezed, letting the thorns prick her palm and send bright signals of pain to her brain.

She could feel herself giving over to the panic, spiraling into worry and terror and paranoia that Chetney was there, right behind her in the brush.

Closing her eyes, Aleah tried to force her breathing to even out, but her breaths would only come in short, ragged bursts.

Squeezing the bramble, feeling the sting against her skin, she thought of Jasper. She thought of the way he'd casually ignored her all the way from South Audha to Jekeida when they'd first met, but always offered her food or water at every stop. She thought of Merriam, Leonidas, Campbell, and Calysta, how they loved and accepted and protected her and filled her with so much warmth and happiness she sometimes felt she would explode.

She thought of Kodi and the feral gleam in his eyes that matched hers so well. She thought of his hands on her, sometimes bruising, but always aware of her response to it, always watching her body and her face for signals and pulling back when she needed him to. She thought of the uncharacteristically sweet words that came from his lips as he did utterly filthy things to her, and the way her stomach would flip, the combination of his words and actions making her want to cling to him for all of eternity.

Once she regained control of her breathing and opened her eyes, she released the bramble, wiping her palm against her pants to clear away the drops of blood seeping from the small wounds.

Aleah knew that she *should* remember Illiziana, but all she could recall with clarity was the fear that had ruled so much of her life as a child. Fear and the ever-present need to hide. Hide herself, hide her feelings, hide her wounds.

Hide her abuse.

Swallowing down the emotions that roiled inside her, Aleah refocused on the estate, pushing everything else aside and concentrating on the job ahead.

Complete the kill. Then she could try to deal with the past that kept threatening to rise up and overwhelm her now that she was back in the city that had tried so hard to bury her.

Aleah waited until the moons had drifted across the sky before getting up and walking toward the overseer's home. She removed her cloak before she entered the property, not wanting to worry about having to hide the billowy extra fabric should she need to make any quick moves.

Scaling the fence with ease, Aleah dropped to the ground below, landing softly and watching for any movement around her.

All was quiet, so she crept forward, liquid and light like a cat. Climbing the tree, she slipped in through the same window as before.

Once inside, Aleah took a moment to listen to the ambient noises in the house. Pipes groaned softly. A clock ticked from somewhere down the hall, muffled but rhythmic. A rogue gust of wind whistled past the windows.

But no creaking of floors or patter of footsteps. No voices, hushed or otherwise. Aleah moved, pausing before each corner to listen for activity, until she was at Illiziana's bedchamber door. It was locked, but she pulled a small kit from her belt and made quick work of it, slipping inside and locking it behind her.

The large, open antechamber was completely silent. Aleah rolled her neck, slipping a dagger from her belt. The viciously curved blade glinted in the moonlight. Aleah flipped it in her hand, the knife jutting from below her pinky. Her thumb traced over the grooves cut into the hilt, citrus dripping with honey that Mollian had carved for her.

An unexpected surge of warmth filled her, and she bit her cheek to force back an ironic chuckle. Her own flesh and blood had done nothing to protect her, but the king of Sekha personalized her weapons with her favorite things, with no motive other than friendship.

Fuck flesh and blood, she thought, and then let everything else fade, focusing only on the task ahead.

Aleah crept quietly into the bedroom, the door opening without a sound. She stuck to the shadows, watching the overseer as she slept.

Illiziana was stretched out onto one side, her hair wrapped in silk that matched the gown on her body.

Aleah approached her, breathing softly through her nose as she placed her feet carefully on the lush carpet. Reaching over the fae's sleeping form, she pressed the end of her knife against Illiziana's neck, taking a quick breath to ready herself for the deep, fast pull across the throat to make the kill quiet and relatively quick and painless.

Illiziana's eyes flicked open a heartbeat after the cool blade touched her throat. Her hand shot up, grabbing Aleah's wrist and twisting hard. The knife nicked her, opening a line against the dark skin of her neck that quickly became a trickle of blood.

Aleah gasped, pain shooting up her arm as her hand opened involuntarily, dropping the knife. Her heart thundered in her chest as Illiziana sat up, keeping a tight hold on her wrist, bent only a short turn away from snapping. Aleah reached for another knife, but Illiziana twisted her wrist, halting her movements with another burst of pain.

"I would think twice bef—Legends above. Aleah?"

Aleah's eyes widened, and she met Illiziana's shocked stare. "You know me?"

Illiziana's grip tightened, but her voice was soft with grief. "You look so much like your uncle—like your mother."

Aleah whimpered at the agonizing strain in her wrist, but cold fear seeped into her bones.

"Spiro told us you drowned in the harbor. I thought you were dead," she whispered quietly, her eyes still wide and unbelieving.

Aleah's mind was racing, trying to piece together a way out without a broken wrist.

Blood still trickled from the cut on Illiziana's throat, soaking into the top of her nightgown, but she didn't pay any attention to it. "I had always thought that maybe he'd finally taken it a step too far, that he'd—" Illiziana broke off, shaking her head in wonder.

She made a horrible, fatal mistake then, and released her hold on Aleah, whose own eyes were now wide and unbelieving, breathing shallowly as her vision swam and blood rushed in her ears. But not loudly enough to drown out what Illiziana said next.

"I guess you finally left, then."

Aleah's vision snapped into focus, tunneling into the fae in front of her as the weight of her words sunk in. *She knew.* All those years of abuse, and Illiziana knew and had stood by and let it happen.

A small smile pulled at the corners of Illiziana's lips. "You're a survi-"

Fury boiled up fast and hot through Aleah, and in one fluid movement, almost too fast to track, she'd freed a second knife from her belt, swinging it up and across the overseer's throat so that her last word was cut off into a gurgling cough, confusion filling those bright blue eyes as she raised her hands to her throat, trying to stop the bleeding.

Thanks to the curve of the blade, the cut was deep, both severing arteries and cutting into the windpipe.

Aleah's mouth was set, her eyes holding Illiziana's gaze as she bled out, blood spilling through her fingers and down the front of her chest. Aleah watched, unmoving, as Illiziana's eyes lost focus, too much blood pouring too quickly, even for her fae healing to mend.

"Fuck you," Aleah hissed as Illiziana collapsed against the headboard, struggling to breathe. She watched until the overseer gave one last, pathetic shudder as her final breath left her body, then grabbed her fallen knife from the bed, moving into the bathroom to rinse the blades. She wanted no trace of that enabling bitch left on her weapons.

Her heart pounded a solid, fast rhythm in her chest that had nothing to do with the murder or her physical exertion as she returned to the inn. The knowledge that others had known what Chetney did to her made her entire body feel like it was on fire.

She wanted to scream. She wanted to rip something apart.

She wanted to run far, far away and never come back. Her whole body shook with energy and emotion by the time she made it back to the inn, the horizon lightening with dawn.

Aleah climbed the side of the building—no need to have someone know she'd showed up at a strange hour—and rolled through the window. Landing on her back on the floor, she pushed her hands into her hair and pulled heavily at the roots until pain bloomed across her scalp.

Others had known.

Others had known and done nothing to save her.

With that had also come the cold, hard truth that she'd always feared. Kinbriars were untouchable.

People with some form of political power had been aware of what was happening behind closed doors, yet no one had come forward. Her family held that much sway in the south.

The thought made her stomach turn, and she rolled over, lurching to her feet and sprinting to the bathroom. She dropped to her knees in front of the toilet, everything in her stomach surging up in a violent, burning wave.

Jasper, woken by the sound, came and knelt beside her, rubbing her back comfortingly.

When she had nothing left to give, Aleah wiped her sleeve across her mouth, sagging into him. "Nothing he did even matters ... he was always going to get away with all of it."

Chapter 12

We're brothers

Fourteen years before …

THE SUN ROSE, SLOWLY eating away the darkness in the open barracks where Jasper lay, wings tucked beneath his shoulders to keep from spilling over the sides of the bed.

He stared at the bunk above him, his jaw aching from clenching his teeth all night. He hadn't slept at all, rage roiling in his blood, his mind spinning things over and over until finality sat in his gut like a stone, his mind made up.

All his life, he'd romanticized the Royal Guard. They were Sekha's protectors, the best of the best, the champions of the common folk. So when he'd been given the opportunity to join, he'd jumped on it without hesitation, ready to sign his life away in the name of helping the helpless.

But the closer he got to completing his training, the more uneasy he felt. He'd seen guardsmen around Umbra bending the very laws they were meant to uphold, corruption rampant in the upper ranks. Ferrick's inner circle were the worst of the bunch, exuding an entitled attitude and viewing the people of Umbra by what they could do for the Guard instead of the other way around.

It was despicable, and he'd grown tired of trying to stomach it.

He stood, grabbing a set of clothes and walking to the showers, flexing his jaw to relieve the tension there. Only a few others were awake, and Jasper stretched out his wings in the space of the nearly empty showers, letting water cascade down his skin, clearing his mind and solidifying his decision.

Turning off the water, he dragged a towel over his head, hair cropped close to his scalp, and over the rest of his body. He gave his wings a hard flutter, droplets spinning from the black feathers.

After dressing, Jasper ate a quick breakfast before making his way to the training room, well into his warm-ups by the time all the other Guard trainees arrived.

"Early morning?"

Jasper turned, bowing his head in deference when he saw the heir apparent. "Couldn't sleep."

Oren tied a band around his head to keep his short, white waves from falling into his eyes while he trained. "Only a few more weeks and you'll be out of the training barracks. I've heard the beds are better for the fully initiated Guard."

Jasper scoffed.

Oren's deep green eyes clouded in confusion. "Ranger training will only take a year, you won't be—"

"I'm not worried about a bed," Jasper interrupted him.

Oren blinked, searching his friend's face. "What happened?"

"Nothing. Everything," he answered with a sharp sigh, looking everywhere but at the prince. "There's a lot you don't see from the castle."

"You know that's not fair." Oren stepped closer to him, lowering his voice as a few more people came into the room. "I thought we were beyond that." His eyes narrowed in a wounded glare, the message in them clear: *don't start treating me like they do.*

"I'm sorry; I'm just frustrated," Jasper apologized, knowing he should say more. But a commander walked into the room, calling the area to order.

Training was brutal that morning, but possibly felt more so because Jasper was tired—physically and mentally. But he kept all those emotions buried, not letting his contempt shine through the bright silver of his eyes. They finished the morning routine with sparring, and Jasper was thoroughly exhausted by the end, having burnt off most of his frustration and more resolved for it.

A few of the recruits were talking about the night prior as they did their cool-down stretches, teasing each other about missed exploits or lost bets. Jasper stood apart from them, his memories of the last night, and many others, filled with different images.

"I need to sneak out more often. I hate missing out on everything."

"You like your beauty sleep too much," Jasper teased.

Oren sat in a crouch, one leg stretched in front of him. He shrugged, smiling as he pulled his leg back in. "Yeah, I won't argue there."

"How do you manage it?" Jasper asked, wiping sweat from his brow.

Oren looked up, sitting back on his heels. "Why do I feel like you're about to take this conversation somewhere entirely deeper?"

"How do you live knowing the very rules that keep society intact are rules that let so many people get away with doing horrible things?"

Oren nodded, pressing his mouth into a thin line. "Is it intuition? Or do I just know you too well?"

Jasper tossed his practice sword aside, leaning one shoulder against the wall. "I'm glad you feel privileged enough to take everything so lightly, Prince."

"I'm sorry, Jaz. I'm here." Oren stood from his crouch, dusting off his pants. "And I live knowing that one day I will have the power to right those wrongs. I just have to bide my time."

"You don't fear that the responsibility of keeping your society from crumbling will overshadow the responsibility you have to your people as individuals?"

"Worrying over things like that won't change anything. All I can do is trust that my values will remain the same. Plus, I'll have Mollian to help with some of the day-to-day stuff. I won't forget whose backs my kingdom is built on," Oren said confidently.

Jasper wet his lips, trying to hold on to tact. "I don't mean to offend, you know that. But, Oren, you don't see everything that goes on. When you're king, you'll see even less. Everyone is always on their best behavior around you because they know that you were born to power."

"I can read people." Oren rolled his eyes. "You don't think I see how Ferrick claws his way into higher and higher standing? How there's not a single neck he won't step on to get what he wants?"

"It's not just Ferrick," Jasper said, folding his arms over his chest.

Oren walked off, stooping to pick up Jasper's discarded sword.

"Well, what do you want me to do about it, Jasper?" he asked defensively. "I'm trying my best to establish a rule that is fair and just. There's not much else I can do aside from follow my own morals and hope to set that example and expectation of those under me."

"Not everything is black and white." Jasper followed him, rubbing a hand across the back of his neck. "That's all I'm trying to say."

Oren turned, throwing his arms out, a sword in each hand. "Don't you get it? Everything I do has to be white. I don't get to pick and choose when to be moral and when to bend the rules. The rules govern society and the rules govern me."

"But the rules don't govern those at the top of the food chain. The rules bend for them."

"Well, they shouldn't."

"They will. Always."

The two stood, staring at each other for a long moment.

"Not everyone has the privilege to see the world without gray, brother." Jasper took the swords from Oren, putting them up.

"Jasper," Oren started, but Jasper held up his hand, shaking his head.

"Are you busy for supper?" he asked.

Oren pulled the band from around his head, white waves spilling free to cover the aspen branches tattooed on his temples. "Nothing special planned that I can think of."

"Let's go on a hike."

Oren eyed him suspiciously. "Why not for lunch?"

"I have plans."

"Don't do something you'll regret, Jaz," the prince pleaded. "Some decisions can't be unmade." He could feel that something had shifted, and it scared him.

"You're right. Some decisions are irreversible, but inevitable all the same." The corner of Jasper's mouth quirked up in the semblance of a smile.

"You don't want to talk first?" Oren asked. And, though he was three years younger, he felt a need to protect Jasper, to vet his decisions the same way he might with Mollian.

"Meet me for supper," Jasper insisted.

"Outside the gates?" Oren challenged.

Jasper nodded.

Oren's jaw set, his eyes searching Jasper's face before he finally nodded. "I'll be there."

Jasper went back to the barracks, taking a quick shower before checking the duty roster. One patrol, then just basic barrack maintenance. More training before supper, but he wasn't planning to be around for that.

After what Jasper had witnessed last night, and not for the first time, he knew he would never be able to stand by, to follow orders rather than letting his own morals dictate his life. He'd spent his childhood in East Eyko, along the coast, and had seen so much. That's why he'd traveled to Umbra to join the Royal Guard. He'd wanted to be able to make a difference in the world and stop all of the evil he saw around him.

But he was only weeks out from pledging his life in servitude to the Crown, and he'd grown more uneasy about it by the day.

Eventually, he'd be a Ranger.

Eventually, he'd make commander.

Eventually, he would have some say or weight in his assignments and some autonomy over what decisions he made and how he chose to handle injustices.

Eventually.

And he'd decided early that morning, before the sun's light had peeked over the mountains, he was no longer okay with eventually.

So, after completing all of his duties for the day, he packed up the few things he owned that hadn't been issued to him by the Guard, stopped into the commander's office attached to the recruits' quarters, and officially resigned.

He stood outside the castle gates with almost nothing to his name and no real knowledge of where he would stay now, but there was a distinct lack of weight hanging on his shoulders, and he felt like he could breathe for the first time in a long time.

Jasper secured a room at an inn in town and stopped by a tavern for some sandwiches before making his way back up to the castle to meet with Oren. The prince walked through the gates at the same time Jasper reached them.

"Impeccable timing, as always." Oren smiled, but worry clouded his eyes.

"Come on, let's climb up to watch the sunset."

Oren flashed him a smile. "If you're trying to romance me, Jaz, I must admit that I see you too much as family, but am flattered nonetheless."

Jasper rolled his eyes, heading up the mountain. "I have no interest in navigating the politics that would come with being the king's consort, Your Highness."

They kept a brisk pace, finally finding an outcrop of rock to sit on that showed them an unhindered view of Umbra. Jasper dangled his legs over the edge, pulling the sandwiches from his pack and tossing one to Oren. They ate in silence for a while before Jasper finally spoke. "I saw a lot of things growing up by the sea."

Oren turned his gaze to him, staying silent.

"Some places are so far removed from the eyes of Umbra and the laws here. People get bold; they make their own laws. Trafficking of drugs and weapons and people, thievery, murder ... I'm not saying everyone accepts it, but it happens. My father worked on the docks, logging imports and exports for the harbormaster. I started working with him when I was twelve, counting crates and running communications between the docks and the porthouse, and it didn't take me long to realize that every luxury I'd ever experienced had been ill-begotten. We weren't rich, by any means, but my family rarely wanted for anything, and it was all thanks to my father's position."

"He accepted bribes?" Oren guessed.

Jasper nodded, staring out over the royal city. "It wasn't the fishermen, the farmers, or the foreign merchants who asked him to miscount goods to avoid taxes. It was the smugglers, barely even pretending to be tradesmen as a guise to hide what they were really moving." His silver eyes darkened with memory, his voice growing quiet. "My father knew which ships were which and tried to keep me from being involved with any of the smugglers. I still don't know whether that was to protect me or to make it easier for him to convince himself that I didn't know what was happening. But one day, when he was busy handling paperwork with another merchant, I started inventory on another ship in his section of the port. I thought maybe he'd be proud of my initiative."

Jasper's throat threatened to close, everything about that day still so vivid in his mind's eye, and he swallowed hard before continuing. "There were kids in that boat, Oren. All dirty and roped together ... I ran back to the deck to get my dad, to get harbor security, but one of the smugglers caught me first. I think he panicked, which is probably the only reason I'm alive. He knocked me over the head and tossed me overboard.

"The wings throw people off, but I was a harbor kid, swimming even before I could fly. My head hurt, and I was bleeding, but I kept below the water until I'd swam behind another boat. How I made it home is a little foggy, but I got myself there, and when my father came home ... he was angry, mostly at himself, but also that I'd boarded a ship without his permission. I tried to tell him what I saw, but he cut me off. He said ... he said it wasn't our business, that we need to know when to keep out of things that don't concern us. We weren't the ones in charge. We had no power. Our safety and prosperity were dependent on our ability to turn a blind eye and keep our mouths shut. That was the first and last time we ever talked about anything that happened on the docks."

Oren leaned his shoulder into Jasper, and he let himself take comfort in the touch. "I never forgot those kids, and I didn't think like my father. I was just a kid myself, and there was nothing I could do with smuggled cargo, but I'd sneak onto ships at night anyway, checking for people, marking the smugglers' ships so they were easier to spot and maybe another port could take them down. A few times I got caught sneaking around the docks at night, and took a good amount of discreet beat-downs by harbor security or crewmen, but that only helped teach me how to fight."

"Did nobody ever try to speak up?" Oren asked, his stomach churning. "Any of the adults who worked the docks, who knew what was happening and had the responsibility to stop it. The Guard has outposts. We send envoys to check with the port cities ..."

Jasper shrugged. "I've seen people try to take action through the proper channels, but everything takes so much time when it's wrapped up in politics. And the people who hold the power? Sometimes they're the most despicable of all."

Oren folded his lips together, wanting to speak up but sensing there was more Jasper needed to get off his chest.

"I joined the Guard because I thought that was a way I could fight all the injustice I'd seen, but I was wrong." Jasper met Oren's gaze. "Even those closest to the law seem to find ways around it."

"Report them, Jasper. My mother would never stand—"

"It's not that simple," Jasper interrupted him. "Once you're labeled as a rat, that's all you'll ever be seen as. Forget promotion, forget ever having a say in what you'll do with your life. I know you and your family are just, but you cannot be everywhere at once, and you're still held to the same laws you're meant to enforce."

Oren's brow furrowed in confusion.

"I want to help people. I want to be free to fight against any injustice and make my own rules, pick my own battles, let my own morals find their hold and learn what lines I am or am not willing to cross." Jasper sighed, looking back out over Umbra. "I can't do that under the Crown's thumb."

"I don't understand what you're saying," Oren said.

Jasper spread his wings, letting the wind that rolled up the mountainside ripple against his feathers, savoring the strain of the muscles in his back as his wings resisted the push of the air. "I'm going to make my living helping people. People I choose to help, in whatever way I feel is just."

Oren couldn't help the laugh that pulled from his throat. "Judge, jury, and executioner, then?"

Jasper shrugged. "You make it seem like the lines are so clear, but I don't see it that way. The world is full of gray."

"If you would let me help you, I could give you the power to make a difference."

"I don't need your power, Oren. And don't you see? Without being held to the rule of the Guard, I can come to you. I can have more freedom to tell you the things that I know without fear of reprisal."

"You quit the Guard today," Oren said.

Jasper nodded. "I'm going to become a mercenary. I have skills that can help people. Skills that were mine even before the Guard cultivated them into something sharper. But I wanted to tell you all of this, because I want you to understand. I know things will change between us now, but they were always going to—you're going to be king. But this way ... this way I can help you, be your eyes and ears outside of the castle and an unbiased opinion should there ever be a time when things get dicey."

"For a price?" Oren eyed him with a smirk.

Jasper chuckled. "Yes, for a price, if you want help getting rid of problems. A male's gotta eat, after all."

"You're wrong though, Jasper."

Jasper turned to him, raising a dark brow in question.

"Things don't have to change between us." Oren met his gaze, sincerity in his deep green eyes. "You were the first person to ever treat me like an equal. Like I'm not just a young prince who deserves deference because I will one day rule. That's why we're friends, and that doesn't change because you don't work for my family anymore. If anything, you branching out on your own takes away any potential awkwardness."

Without giving himself a chance to overthink it, Jasper embraced Oren, squeezing his eyes shut against the emotion filling him. It had been years since he'd felt connected to another person, able to share his truest thoughts and opinions and feelings. They'd been one another's confidants, the first that either had been able to trust with the things that were in their hearts without fear of judgment or reprisal. "I will miss you, Prince."

Oren's hold tightened around his shoulders before he released him with a laugh. "I won't miss getting pummeled by you every other day in training. But I mean what I said. Don't distance yourself from me just because you're no longer Guard. I still need you." The joke in his voice was undercut with the vulnerability plain on his face, and Jasper nodded, not turning away from it.

"I know this isn't a lifestyle you're able to condone, but I hope you can understand that it's something I have to do. And I swear to you, Oren, you will never have to doubt my loyalty to you. I will never knowingly do anything that would cause detriment to you or to Sekha."

"I know." Oren looked back out over Umbra and knocked his shoulder into Jasper's. "We're brothers, Jaz. Always will be."

Chapter 13

You're insane

KODI SAT ON A **dock**, kicking his feet in the open space between the wood and the water and twirling a knife in his fingers as he contemplated the irreversible turn the day had taken.

Rovin had shown up the night before all out of sorts, because of something that had happened with Merriam. From the sound of things, they were finally starting to dip into admitting that they might feel something for each other, and he happily tucked that information away, knowing it would be a good distraction and source of happiness for Aleah.

But despite Aleah's goal of getting their closest friends together, he knew Merriam had been through a lot and understood better than most the animosity that used to live between her and Rovin. So he'd decided to talk to her, gauge how she was feeling about all of it and, if she seemed open to it, give her a little push toward Rovin. And if he got the sense that she wasn't into growing whatever was festering inside of Rovin, he could gently start trying to push his friend's attention elsewhere.

The conversation had gone better than expected, but any trace of his good mood had been washed away in entirety when Chetney Kinbriar had appeared behind him. His skin still crawled where the heir had touched him, and he tightened his grip on the hilt of his knife as a preternatural stillness settled over his body.

In a single conversation, the heir had proven himself to be the same unapologetically vile creature that haunted Aleah's nightmares, and Kodi's self-restraint had snapped, completely giving over to that predator part of his brain. He released a slow breath from his nose, resuming the swing of his feet and flipping the knife through his fingers as his mouth watered in anticipation.

He'd sent Jasper a message that morning, and all day he'd been wired with energy, every nerve in his body singing as he planned. The sun was sinking below the water in a brilliant burst of pinks and oranges when he heard Jasper land behind him, squatting down with his wings flared for balance.

"I'm going to kill that bastard," Kodi said simply, his eyes locked on an obscenely large board painted with Chetney's likeness.

Jasper knew it wasn't a threat or even an eventuality. It was their last night in Do Lech, and the Ranger was out for blood. "His family owns the largest port in Sekha."

"I couldn't give a fuck what he owns." His knuckles went white with the force of his grip on the knife hilt, and he forced himself to relax, resuming twirling the blade.

"You're a Ranger, Kodi. I only meant that you are held to a high standard and very stringent code of conduct."

Kodi met Jasper's gaze, his bi-colored eyes hard and resolute. "She was just a kid, Jasper. I don't care if I get locked away for the rest of my life. I'm going to remove that scum from the face of Nethyl."

Jasper nodded, turning his eyes back to the giant board. "You love her."

Heat curled through the Ranger, every nerve crackling with violent, vengeful energy. "I do."

Twisted locs of hair fell over one shoulder as Jasper tilted his head. "Have you told her?"

A smile flickered over Kodi's lips. "Once, and I'm sure you can probably guess how she handled that."

Jasper chuckled. "She's never been graceful with intimacy."

Kodi ran his fingers through his mohawk, mussing up the curls. "Little merc has a lot of trauma, and while I love every wild, unhinged inch of who it made her, I will beat the living shit out of the beast who hurt her, along with anyone who tries to stop me."

Jasper rolled his shoulders, tucking in his wings as he stood. He knew there could be repercussions, knew there was a lot of risk, but there wasn't a single part of him that wanted to stop this. As long as Kodi understood what he was doing, Jasper would eagerly assist. "Shall I kidnap an overseer's heir, then?"

Kodi's lips pulled back from his teeth in a horrifyingly feral smile. "Let's grab us a child abuser."

They briefly discussed the plan, then Jasper flew off, and Kodi pulled the hood of his cloak up over his head, making sure the sleeves of his shirt were pulled down to cover his Ranger tattoos, and walked through town.

The brightly lit streets with outlandishly decorated buildings gave way to quiet suburbs, and then to older, more rundown businesses along the bay. A certain block had been hit hard by an intense storm a few years back, and instead of rebuilding, the businesses had all relocated, leaving a stretch of vacant, dilapidated structures.

Kodi had scoped out the area earlier in the day, and now climbed onto some old crates stacked against one of the vacant buildings, jumping to grab hold of the end of a rusted metal fire escape and swinging his legs expertly onto the landing. The metal groaned under his weight, but years of scouting and climbing far less sturdy structures kept his feet confident, and he climbed to a second-story window that was left open, the glass blown out in a storm, and hopped inside.

He slipped down to the basement, checking his previous set up, then walked back up to the main floor, dusting his hands off on his pants in anticipation.

Jasper's footfalls came moments later, and Kodi looked to the top of the stairs to see him pulling a fae, wrists bound together in iron, after him.

Muffled noises came from the sack-covered head, and Jasper gave Kodi a grim smile before tugging the fae down the stairs after him. A more insistent noise came from the male at the motion, and he took a step forward, falling to his knees with an angry cry.

Jasper jerked him back to his feet. "Watch your step there, Kinbriar."

Kodi helped Jasper bring Chetney down to the basement, stretching his arms out and securing each wrist to an iron chain bolted into the wall.

With Chetney secured, Kodi pulled the hood from his head, relishing in the livid glare of those bright hazel eyes. Chetney's freckled cheeks were ruddy with anger as he attempted to scream insults and threats through the gag stuffed into his mouth, filling Kodi with dark amusement. "Hey, calm down there for a second. I'll pull that gag from your mouth, but you look pretty irate. I'm gonna warn you, if you try to bite me, I do bite back."

Chetney's breaths came hard and fast through his nose, anger still plain on his face.

"I know you're probably not used to taking instructions, lordling," Jasper added mockingly, "but I would highly suggest you not try to call him on any bluffs."

Kodi reached to pull the balled fabric from Chetney's mouth, and as soon as it was free, Chetney snapped his head forward, gnashing his teeth.

Kodi's head dropped back in a laugh. "Oh, you want to prove something right now?" His bi-colored eyes gleamed in the low light as he crooked a finger, holding it in front of Chetney's face. "Go on, sink your teeth in and I'll do the same to your cheek. Whoever holds on the longest wins."

Chetney met Kodi's gaze, and a bit of the fight guttered out of his eyes as he pinched his lips together and swallowed.

"Please, test me." Kodi shoved his finger against Chetney's mouth.

The fae whipped his head to the side angrily. "You're fucking sick."

"Glad we both have each other pinned so well! I am sick, I'll give you that, and you're a low-life, piece of shit child abuser who's about to *really* regret his life choices."

"What the fuck are you on about? My home is teeming with Royal Guard; they'll know I'm missing by now! They'll find me!"

Kodi roughly pushed his sleeves up, the material bunching over his elbows, and raised one arm to Chetney's eye-level. "I'm well aware the Guard are at the estate."

The sight of Kodi's Ranger tattoo sparked a fresh wave of desperation, and Chetney tugged against the iron chains looped over his wrists. "You will hang for this!"

Kodi rolled his eyes, glancing behind him to Jasper. "Are you going to turn me in?"

Jasper cocked his head to the side, folding his arms over his chest.

"I haven't seen anything tonight other than a Ranger conducting routine Ranger business."

Kodi turned back to Chetney, twirling the tip of a dagger against the pad of his finger. "Empty threat then."

"You can't just pull citizens from the street and threaten them. Do you have any idea who I am? My family owns this town!"

Kodi's eyes darkened, and he pressed the blade against Chetney's cheek and cut a line down the skin. "I know exactly who your family is, Chet. I would say that your niece sends her regards, but she refused to even set foot in the city proper. Now why do you think that is?"

The sting across Chetney's cheek was completely overpowered by surprise, his lips moving soundlessly for a moment before he scoffed. "She's alive, then? Whatever that halfling bitch is paying you, I can triple it."

Kodi arched a brow, pausing for a moment at the sheer audacity before a dark chuckle spilled from his chest. "Oh, it's going to be *so* good to hear you scream."

"If you hurt me, my family will tell the king," he threatened, changing tactics as the color drained from his face.

Kodi leaned in close. "I hope they do. He'll have them executed for what they let you do to his *mehhen's* best friend," he said before drawing his tongue up the cut on Chetney's cheek. He leaned back and spit the blood back in the fae's face.

Chetney started shaking then.

"Smart of you to finally look scared," Jasper spoke, spreading his wings as he took a step toward him. "Though you are far past the point of any mercy."

"Do you remember the scars you gave her, Chet? Did you get pleasure from marring her skin?" Kodi leaned in close, eyes lit with savage delight. "Because Legends know I got pleasure from memorizing every single one. Tracing them with my fingers and my tongue until they were burned into my brain, until my hands could repeat the path they carve across her body from muscle memory."

The fae swallowed, tilting his head back and away. "I was grief stricken. My sister—my *mehhen*—y-you don't know what it's like to lose someone so close to you, so much a part of you."

Kodi ignored him, trailing the tip of his knife down Chetney's neck and back up into his hair. "Lucky for you, I find those scars so fucking pretty. Because guess what, Chet? You get to match." As the last word left his mouth, Kodi sliced the blade over the tip of Chetney's ear, the tapered point falling to the ground and a deep furrow welling blood where the knife cut into his scalp.

Chetney was screaming, a string of blubbering nonsense falling from his lips as he begged and pleaded to be let go.

"Actually, you'll only partially match my little merc." Kodi paid no attention to his cries. "I like to think I'm a bit of a creative, and, Chetty-boy, I'd be lying if I said I haven't dreamed of this moment on more than one occasion." With that, Kodi cut the tip off of Chetney's other ear, and a wet, anguished cry filled the room.

Jasper rested a hand on Kodi's shoulder. "Signal me when you're done."

Kodi nodded, not taking his eyes from Aleah's uncle, but registering Jasper's departure. The mercenary would take care of Aleah, and Kodi would be free to inflict revenge on her tormentor, who continued to cry out with fervor. "Legends, fuck, stop your screaming." Kodi backhanded Chetney, cutting him off mid-wail. "You want to live, right? A chance to make things right?"

Chetney's hazel eyes widened with relief. "Yes! Yes, I'll make it right, I swear!"

Kodi tapped the tip of his knife against his chin for a moment before flipping it around and sliding it into his belt. "All right, Lord Kinbriar, I'll make a deal with you. Would you say you're an honorable male?"

"Yes!" Chetney gasped, blood dripping down his shoulders.

"I don't agree, but I do consider *myself* honorable, so here's what'll happen. I'm going to unchain you, and we're going to fight it out in a good old-fashioned duel. I'm sure you've had plenty of fancy combat training."

Chetney's eyes narrowed, tears still streaming down his face. "What? No, that's not fair! You're a Ranger!"

Anger flooded Kodi's blood, and dark, manic laughter spilled from his chest. He tilted his head to the side, gripping Chetney's chin and meeting his gaze. "Not fair?" He laughed. "It's not *fair*?" Kodi curled his nails into Chetney's cheeks, applying pressure that forced the fae's jaws apart.

Abruptly, he ripped his hand away, digging shallow furrows into Chetney's skin in the process. "I guess you're right, Chet. It wouldn't be fair." He unclasped Chetney, who instinctively raised shaking hands to his ears, sobbing when his fingers brushed blood.

Kodi slid his knife from his belt, flipping it over, catching it by the flat of the blade and holding it out to Chetney. "Take it," he insisted, annunciating each syllable.

Unsure whether or not it was a trick, Chetney hesitated briefly before grabbing it, his palms slick with blood and sweat and his throat dry from fear.

"Now you're armed, and I've got nothing but my fists." Kodi held his arms out and twirled, showing his lack of weapons. "Fight me," he ordered, every ounce of amusement disappearing from his voice.

Chetney swallowed once and then lunged. Kodi easily dodged. When Chetney lunged again, Kodi stuck his foot out, tripping him.

"Is that the best you've got, Lord Kinbriar?" Kodi taunted.

Chetney scrambled to his feet, sliding in the blood that had dripped onto the floor. He lashed out at Kodi, who knocked his hand away and threw a fist into the center of his abdomen. Chetney coughed, sinking to one knee and holding his stomach.

"Get up and fight me," Kodi commanded.

Once again, Chetney lunged to his feet, swiping the knife at Kodi. The Ranger dipped out of the way, bringing his foot up solidly into Chetney's crotch.

Chetney fell to his knees with a cry, the knife falling from his hands as he cupped his balls.

"FIGHT ME!" Kodi screamed at him, letting out a wild lash of magic that shook the room. He sank down to peer into Chetney's eyes, grabbing a fistful of red hair to yank his head back and force eye contact. "You know why this fight could never be *fair*?" He leaned forward until his forehead was almost touching Chetney's. "It's not fair, to you, at least, because I'm not a child who's unable to fight back, you sick fuck." With that, Kodi tilted his head back and rocked it forward, his hairline connecting with Chetney's nose.

A loud crack filled the room only a heartbeat before Chetney screamed, bringing his hands up to his face as blood poured down his chest.

Kodi laughed, standing and raising a hand to wipe at the blood trickling down his forehead where his skin split from the impact.

"You're a fucking psychopath!" Chetney screeched, cradling his face. "You'll hang for this, you fucking freak!"

"Yeah, you keep saying that." Kodi grabbed Chetney's wrist, wrenching it away from his face and securing it back in chains before doing the same with the other. Chetney struggled, but was too weak from pain to put up much of a fight.

Kodi ripped off Chetney's shirt, revealing smooth, freckled skin free of any major blemish. "What a canvas," he purred, running his fingers down the fae's chest. Revulsion raised the hair on the back of his neck, but it mixed with a deep pleasure at the look of absolute terror on Chetney's face.

"Stop, please, I can pay you. I can give you anything you want," Chetney whimpered in a last-ditch effort for mercy, all bravado gone as Kodi leaned down to pick up the knife.

"What I *want* is for Aleah to go where she pleases without fear of who she might run into, to know without a shadow of a doubt that you will *never* be able to touch her again." Kodi drew the tip of the knife down Chetney's chest, his voice shaking with restraint.

"I won't," Chetney coughed. "I won't ever touch her again! I swear it on every Legend."

Kodi smiled, flicking his eyes up to meet Chetney's pleading gaze. "I know."

Chetney trembled, swallowing down a scream as Kodi drew the knife across his skin. Even when Chetney again started screaming, Kodi paid him no mind, just methodically worked the knife, some cuts long and shallow, others short and deep. By the time he was finished, blood coated the floor, and Chetney sagged against his restraints, his throat raw.

Kodi stood back, tapping the bloodied blade of the knife against his palm as he surveyed his handiwork. He gave a small nod, a smile playing at the corner of his lips, before he leaned forward to clean the blade on Chetney's pants.

Slipping the knife back into his belt, Kodi grabbed a cup of water from the bench to the side of the room, walking it over and holding it to Chetney's lips.

The fae drank, slowly at first, then more eagerly, his body trembling and water spilling over his chin.

His ears and nose had stopped bleeding about halfway through Kodi's carving. The magic in his blood couldn't be wielded because of the iron around his wrists, but it still did what it could to heal his wounds.

When the water was gone, Kodi leaned back against the wall with a heavy sigh. "I should've seen this coming, Chet, but the marks just don't hit the same as Aleah's do." He tsked. "Now, we could excuse that with the fact that yours are fresh and hers are decidedly not. They've had, what, a decade on her skin? Longer? But even with that much time passed, I just don't think you'll ever match her level of beauty."

Chetney wet his lips, hazel eyes bright with fear and pain. "That much time ... does that ... does that mean I will live?"

Kodi laughed, tossing his head back. "The fuck? Absolutely not. Your body needed a breather for what comes next, though. I can't have you tapping out on me for this."

Chetney swallowed, shaking his head. "No, please. I've learned my lesson. I swear I've learned." The words fell from him in weak cries.

Kodi snorted. "Lesson? You're not doing yourself any favors running your mouth, Chet. Did you really need a *lesson* to understand you don't physically abuse a child? Your own flesh and blood, nonetheless. Fucking Legends above. And somehow *I'm* the psychopath in this scenario?"

"Please," Chetney whispered, tears and snot streaming down his face. "Please."

"Begging's not my kink, buddy," Kodi replied with no emotion, pulling his knife back out and walking behind Chetney. Taking a deep breath, Kodi harnessed his magic, feeling it surge through the corded muscles of his arms, back, and chest. "Try not to scream, yeah? Save your energy," Kodi advised, placing the tip of his knife against Chetney's spine and drawing a smooth line right alongside the knobs of his backbone.

The tip of Kodi's tongue poked from between his teeth as he slid the blade into the wound, methodically working his way down Chetney's back as he separated skin from muscle.

The pain rolled through Chetney in a more powerful wave than he'd ever imagined possible, and everything in his stomach surged up his throat, spewing from his mouth.

Kodi grimaced at the sound of vomit splattering across the floor, wrinkling his nose against the smell of bile and partially digested food. "That's just gross," he mumbled, keeping his hand steady as he skinned Chetney's back.

With the skin sufficiently separated, Kodi drew it back, letting it hang in two flaps before he reached around to pat Chetney's cheek. "You still with me?" A strangled whimper answered him, and he smiled. "Try to stay awake, okay?"

Kodi pressed the tip of his blade against the top of a rib and, using his magic to add force behind the movement, sunk it into Chetney's flesh and pulled down, cracking through the bone. A scream, louder and more desperate than anything Kodi had ever heard, filled the room. He acknowledged the pleasure that warmed his blood at the sound, knowing who it came from.

"You deserve so much worse," he muttered. Kodi continued without stopping after that, breaking through each rib before pulling the bones away from the spine, spreading them behind Chetney's back.

The fae beneath him had long gone silent, but his heart was still beating, albeit feebly, when Kodi exposed his lungs. Kodi pulled each one free in turn, stringing them up to Chetney's splayed arms using lengths of intestine to secure them.

By the time he finished, Kodi was covered in blood and breathing heavily from the strain of tearing apart and rearranging Chetney's body, and Chetney was dead, his head hanging limply down to his chest, his lungs and ribs spread as wings behind him.

Kodi wiped the back of his hand across his mouth, nodding as he surveyed what he'd done. Then he set the knife down and climbed the stairs, leaving bloody footprints on the wood. He climbed up to the second floor, lighting a candle and placing it in a window to signal Jasper that he was done, then walked back to the main floor, turning on the tap in the kitchen and washing off his hands, arms, and face.

He was drying off his arms with a towel, contemplating what to do about his clothes, when he heard movement upstairs.

"Now will you tell me what the fuck is going on? Why are you being so secreti—Kodi?" Aleah appeared at the top of the staircase.

He lowered the towel, smiling in greeting. "Hey, pretty thing," he drawled, tension leaving his body as he looked at her.

Her eyes went wide when she noticed the blood on his clothes, and she leapt down the stairs, landing at the bottom and springing to her feet. "Are you okay?" She raced toward him, and he caught her by the shoulders with a soft chuckle.

"I'm fine. It's not mine," he assured her, letting her fall against him, her arms winding tight around his waist.

Jasper slowly descended the stairs, leaning against the banister.

Kodi took a deep breath, pushing her back. He held the sides of her face, looking into her eyes before leaning forward to rest his forehead against hers. His thumbs brushed her cheeks, and his eyes closed as he breathed in her air. The full weight of how much he loved her tightened his chest to an almost painful degree. "Legends, you've got me fucked beyond repair, Aleah."

She smiled, resting her hands against his wrists. "You're *going* to be fucked beyond repair if you don't tell me what we're doing in an abandoned building in the dead of night."

Kodi pulled back so he could meet her gaze again. "Chetney's dead. He'll never touch you again."

Aleah's eyes went wide, her mouth popping open. "What? I don't—" Her gaze dropped from Kodi's face to his blood-soaked clothes.

He stood still, letting her take the time to process everything.

"You ... you killed him?" Her eyes drifted back up to his.

He nodded, expression neutral as he watched her.

Aleah licked her lips, trying to decipher the emotions that flooded her system. Strongest and loudest was relief. Every beat of her heart was like a new surge of hope. She'd lived for so long in fear of having to see him again, in fear of having to endure the weight of his stare as he looked at her and saw an imperfect version of her mother, flawed and tainted and weak. But now ...

"Why?" The question came out soft and subdued.

Kodi swallowed, emotion flaring behind his eyes. "Because he hurt you."

Aleah bit her lip, seeing plainly in his face what he wanted to say, but wouldn't. *Because I love you.* She took a deep, shuddering breath, steeling her spine as she asked for something she wasn't positive she wanted. "Can I see him?"

Kodi nodded, grabbing her hand.

Jasper had waited to make sure Aleah was comfortable and wouldn't need an escape, but once he felt sure she'd be fine with Kodi, he headed back upstairs, leaving them alone while he left to get Merriam to help move the body.

Kodi led Aleah down to the basement, feeling suddenly nervous as he gripped her hand. He released her when he reached the foot of the stairs, tucking his hands into his pockets.

She stepped forward, her boots squelching softly in the drying blood that coated the floor. Reaching out, she grabbed a handful of flame-red hair, lifting Chetney's head to look into his dull, lifeless eyes. She swallowed hard, waiting for panic to seize her chest and darken her vision. But he was dead, and even though adrenaline flooded her veins being so close to him, she knew he couldn't hurt her. Dropping his head, Aleah choked back a laugh as she took in the rest of the gruesome scene. The laugh caught in her throat, and she raised a shaking hand to cover her mouth as a sob worked its way free. *This is real. He's gone.* Tears lined her eyes as her fingers trailed across her stomach, recognizing the pattern of her scars replicated on Chetney, and a smile played at the corners of her lips. "Kodi, what is this?" She dropped the hand from her mouth to gesture vaguely toward the macabre wings at her uncle's back.

Kodi shrugged, scratching the back of his head. "Art?"

Aleah turned to him. "You're insane."

He tilted his head, studying her. "So I've been told."

"I love you."

His heart skipped a beat, then thundered, and he struggled to catch his breath. "What?" he replied dumbly.

Aleah smiled sheepishly, brushing her hair behind her ear. "I love you."

Kodi launched himself at her, lifting her with his arms around the back of her legs and burying his face in her neck as she squealed. "Say it again."

"I love you," she said with a breathless giggle.

Overwhelmed, he sank his teeth in where her neck met her shoulder, his canines tearing her skin. Blood welled to the surface, and he lapped it up with the flat of his tongue, swallowing with an unrestrained groan. "Damn it, woman, I love you," he whispered against her throat.

"Take me upstairs." Aleah wrapped her legs around his waist. His hands gripped her hips hard enough to bruise as their lips crashed together. Aleah slid her tongue against his to taste the saltiness of her blood that lingered there, tangling her fingers in the back of his hair as she felt him grow hard between them.

Kodi broke the contact only long enough to locate the stairs, and she grinned at his urgency as he walked them back to the main floor. "You're filthy, Ko." She bit his lip, rolling her hips against the length of him, and Kodi groaned, moving one hand to the back of her head and pressing her further against his mouth.

He dropped her on a countertop in the kitchen, and she gripped his chin, pulling back slightly to look into his lust-drunk eyes. "*Filthy* fucking good boy." Aleah let her legs fall, reaching between them to remove his belt and loosen the laces of his pants.

Kodi did the same for her, pulling her pants down below her knees, where they got caught against her boots. A frustrated grunt ripped from him, but Aleah laughed, sliding her palm down the length of his cock and leaning forward to brush her lips against his chin.

"Leave them. I need you." Aleah gripped him, drawing the head of his cock between her legs and situating the tip against her center.

"*Fuck*, you're soaked, little merc." He bracketed her throat with one hand, squeezing as he looked into her eyes and pushed into her. "Safe word?"

"Peaches." Aleah whimpered the word that was their default, her mind too clouded with desire to come up with something witty as she stretched around him, sliding her hands underneath his shirt and dragging her nails across his shoulders. Her hips rocked to meet his measured but punishing thrusts as she clung to him, crashing her mouth back to his and latching onto his lower lip. She bit until she tasted blood, sucking it into her mouth before releasing him. Aleah moved her hands to either side of his head and pressed her lips back to his. Kodi's mouth opened, and, using her tongue, she pushed his blood, diluted with her saliva, into his mouth.

Kodi moaned, pushing roughly into her as he swallowed, sliding his hand around her neck to the back of her head, his other grip bruising against her hip as he held her in place. With her legs trapped by her pants, Aleah's balance on the edge of the counter wasn't the most stable, and Kodi held her to him, desperate and possessive.

"Touch yourself," he said against her lips, voice husky with lust, fingers curling deeper into her skin and his other hand dragging down her back, holding her further in place. Pleasure coiled tight at the base of his spine, each thrust into her fraying the edge of his control.

She slid one hand down between them, her fingers moving across her clit as Kodi angled his hips to more heavily drag against that spot inside of her. He pressed his forehead against hers, looking down to watch himself fuck her and watch her add to her pleasure. "Fuck," he whispered as she clenched around him, feeling her release close.

Aleah dug her nails into his shoulder and made tighter circles against her clit. The stimulation paired with the fullness of him inside her was quickly pushing her over the edge. "Kodi," she whimpered. "I'm gonna come. I'm gonna come on your cock while you're covered in my uncle's blood."

Kodi buried his forehead against her neck. "Does it turn you on knowing my hands were in his chest?" he licked up the column of her throat, thrusting into her. "I know it does. You're so fucking wet and your sweet little cunt is squeezing me so tight because you're thinking about the way I pulled his lungs out of his back." He felt her tighten around him more and pressed his mouth to the base of her neck. "You're fucking *depraved*, little merc." Then he bit her with a low moan.

Aleah's head dropped to the side, the feeling of his teeth and tongue against her skin and that prick of pain tearing her orgasm from her. His name fell from her lips as her release raced through her, starting in her core, curling her toes, and rushing up to her head and darkening the edges of her vision.

Hearing her cry out, Kodi's pace shifted, and within moments, he was slamming into her, following her over the edge. He held her close, licking softly at where he'd broken her skin before finding her mouth and kissing her, languid and satisfied.

As Aleah's heartbeat gradually slowed to a normal rhythm, the weight of Kodi's actions settled in her bones, the gift of retribution she'd never thought possible grounding her in the moment. "Thank you," she breathed.

Kodi rubbed the tip of his nose against hers. "*Nothing* will ever matter more than you. Your happiness, your safety, your needs are my priority. From now until I die." He kissed her again before she could reply, deeply and with promise.

Chapter 14

Stay safe up here

THE PAST COUPLE OF weeks had been slow for Campbell, so he'd been spending his time in the aviary helping Horscha while Leonidas focused on helping Mollian. He was sitting behind the counter, feet kicked up in front of him as he read a book Aleah and Merriam had recommended when the bell above the door tinkled, accompanied by the flap of wings.

"If it isn't the most beautiful boy in all of Sekha." Campbell dropped his feet, leaning his elbows on the counter as Panic landed in front of him. The bird tipped his head forward to brush against Campbell's chin, chirping happily. "How can I help you, sir?" he asked, lifting his gaze to Leonidas with a cheeky smile as he brushed the back of a finger down Panic's chest.

"I've got a job opportunity. Know anyone who's good with his hands?" Leonidas asked, walking around the back of the counter.

Campbell fluttered his lashes. "Well, I'm tempted to offer, but I'm already in a bit of a committed relationship."

"Is that right?" Leonidas slipped a hand through Campbell's curls, grasping the base of an antler and tipping his head back.

"The guy I'm with *really* isn't a fan of other people putting their hands on me," he cautioned, biting his lip at the tantalizing pressure against his skull.

Leonidas leaned down to kiss him. "Worth the risk."

Campbell slid a sly look to Panic. "Smooth talker, this one."

Panic stamped his feet, done with their nonsense, and flew upstairs in search of Horscha and, hopefully, more attention.

"You have a job for me?" Campbell asked, sitting up straighter.

"Only if you're interested in breaking into Ferrick's office."

The fae's indigo eyes widened in surprised delight. "Toeing the line of treason, but make it sanctioned by the king? Absolutely, I have interest."

"He got a letter today. I don't know who it came from, which is the problem. He was already in the aviary waiting for it when I got in this morning, so it was expected."

"And important enough for him to wait around for," Campbell said. "I'll give his office a snoop and see what I can find. Horscha should be almost done closing up shop for the night. Supper first and then I'll head up the hill?"

Campbell walked through the castle gates armed with the excuse of visiting the aviary for Leonidas, but the guardsmen on duty recognized him, letting him through with friendly waves and no questions asked. He wandered toward the aviary before drifting off casually toward the barracks.

The hardest part about becoming unnoticeable had been learning not to care whether or not people noticed him. Some fair folks' animal traits didn't stick out or were easy to hide—Campbell's was not. He'd gone through a phase when first joining a mercenary guild where he'd filed down his antlers in order to better blend in, but it was arduous upkeep and startling every time he saw himself.

It had made him even more conspicuous, because he was so conscious of the fact that he had no antlers to try to hide that he was always touching his hair, wondering if the nubs were poking from his curls. A male with antlers was recognizable, but nowhere near as memorable as a male hanging around places where crimes had happened, acting fidgety and out of place.

Alternatively, nobody recalled seeing someone who looked like they belonged. There was nothing noteworthy about just another person going about their day with the smooth, easy self-assurance of someone who was exactly where they were supposed to be and minding their own business.

So, while Campbell never drew attention to himself, he didn't take drastic measures to keep from being seen outright. And no one noticed as he slipped into the trees behind the barracks, watching the light from Ferrick's office window. He waited until the view went dark, and a few moments after that as the captain left the barracks, then walked up to the window, pulling a lock kit from his belt.

He slipped a thin, long-handled hook between the panes to unlatch them and swung them open, hoisting himself up and over the window ledge. He scoured through the neat stacks of paper on the desk before unlocking the drawers, settling into the desk chair to leaf through the contents. Most of what had been left on the desktop felt pretty standard and mundane—schedules, training regimens, leave requests—but inside the drawers were files of much more interesting documents.

Campbell glanced toward the door, listening for footsteps down the hall, and tossed a look over his shoulder out the window before pulling a penlight from his belt. Merriam had gifted it to him a few years back, grabbing him battery replacements as needed, and it was one of his most prized possessions. He balanced the light between a prong of his antlers, careful to keep the beam of light focused on the papers in front of him as he read over official correspondence from different outposts, potential battle strategies, and enlistment and recruitment statistics. None of this was what he was supposed to be looking for, but he was already there, so he gleaned as much information as he could—never knowing when it might be valuable—before sliding everything neatly back into place and continuing the search.

But nothing came up.

He checked the desk for false bottoms and hidden compartments, scoured the bookshelves, and even moved aside paintings to check for hidden safes. No recent correspondence outside of the couple of mundane letters on the desktop.

Campbell sighed, pulling the flashlight from its perch. Just before he clicked it off, the beam landed on the fireplace and a spot of cream in the sea of light gray ashes. "Hello, there," he whispered with a smile, squatting down to pinch the corner of the paper between his fingers.

He pulled a mostly charred letter from the ashes and shook it clean as best he could. The entire top half of the paper was gone, much of the rest charred beyond readability, including the crest that had been stamped onto the bottom in lieu of a signature.

But there were a few sentences toward the bottom of the page that had remained intact, and they chilled Campbell to the bone.

I will not help you aside from this piece of advice: be careful who else you say these things to, Pos.
Many others would not turn a blind eye to your so-called hypothesizing.

"What are you planning, Captain?" Campbell wondered aloud. He pushed around the other ashes, but found nothing else. So he replaced the bit of correspondence, clicked off his light, and climbed back out the window.

Once he had the latch back in place, he moved into the trees and wandered out near the main path from the castle, heading back toward the barracks. He strolled through the front door casually, hands tucked into his pockets. "Hey, is Bellamy around?" he asked when one of the Rangers playing cards in the common area looked up at him.

The mild interest in her eyes disappeared with the question, and her attention moved back to the game. "Dunno. Might be in his room."

"Thanks." Campbell gave a friendly wave before walking up the stairs to Bellamy's room and rapping lightly on the door.

"It's open."

Campbell pushed the door open and stepped inside.

"Cam? What are you—"

"Good, you're alone," he interrupted, closing the door behind him and moving further into the room. "It felt less conspicuous to find you than to try to talk to Mollian right now. I was just in Ferrick's office, and—"

"You broke into Ferrick's office?" Bellamy's eyes went wide.

Campbell waved his hand dismissively. "That's not impressive. However, it seems like he's been talking to people outside of Jekeida. I don't know who or how many or about what exactly, but it's good you're keeping a closer watch on Ryddan."

Bellamy grew substantially more serious at that. "We're right, then? To be suspicious of the captain?" Some of the light guttered out of his gray-blue eyes, disheartened by the cold truth that someone sworn to protect the Crown so wholly would be capable of something so treasonous. But then the young Ranger's expression hardened. "He won't have a chance to get near Ryddan, and there's no way he'll ever outsmart Molli."

Campbell offered a grim smile. "There's nothing in there to pin him down. Nothing that says what he's planning or even that he's truly planning anything at all, just ... let Mollian know to keep his wits about him." Campbell turned to leave, looking back over his shoulder. "And, Bell? Stay safe up here. If anything happens, Rydd knows where to find us."

Bellamy met his eyes, the air between them heavy with solemnity. Protect the prince. Protect the king. Campbell may not have been sworn to it, but his commitment was no less steadfast. "Thank you," Bellamy said before the mercenary slipped out.

Chapter 15
Tonight we celebrate

CALYSTA HAD SPENT THE majority of her week south among the nymphs. Novi had met with her and shown her all the things that had changed since her last visit, but had remained extremely secretive about why they had actually summoned her.

"I've been planning something with a few of the others," Novi said, drawing their fingers through Calysta's hair. "It will fix everything."

"But what is there to fix?" A frown creased Calysta's brow as her gaze traveled over the forest around them, but nothing seemed amiss.

Novi clicked their tongue against their teeth. "I've said too much already. You'll know when you need to, little 'lysta," they chided, tapping her nose with one claw-tipped finger. "I don't want to jinx fate by spilling the outcome before it's a surety."

Resigned to the secrecy, Calysta sighed, swatting Novi's hand away. "You're too superstitious for your own good."

The night before she would travel north with her friends, Calysta was in the woods to the north of Do Lech, peering through foliage much too dense to be strictly natural. Novi had told her that morning that it was time, and all would be revealed soon. "Was all this really necessary?" she asked the wood nymph beside her.

"Can't have the fae spying in on us, can we?" Novi replied, letting their magic seep out and into the plants, allowing just enough space for the two of them to pass through before rebuilding the wall behind them.

We are fae, Calysta thought with a prick of unease, but quickly shook it off, turning a teasing smile to her friend. "So secretive."

"All for good reason." Novi tossed a smile over their shoulder. "Can't let them all know we're celebrating."

Calysta tipped her head in confusion, but they broke into a clearing before she could ask for clarification.

The meadow was filled with nymphs drinking, dancing, and playing instruments. Light, lively woodwind music filled the space, and Calysta looked around in wonder. It had been many, many years since she'd been to a gathering of so many. Strictly speaking, it wasn't legal.

Thick, leafy vines wove through the trees surrounding the meadow, and a dense layer of humid air hung above, working together to create a sound barrier.

"You spend too much time with the common fae," Novi joked, grabbing Calysta's hand and pulling her further into the meadow. Drinks were pressed into their hands, liquor fermented from and flavored by a medley of fruits, and Calysta soon forgot what there had been to be confused about in the first place.

She danced with Novi, feeling the magic thick in the air and letting her own spin free to entwine with it. She sang and drank and, when her feet finally grew tired, she stumbled away from the din and collapsed happily into the grass.

Novi's long, indigo hair had been braided with bright red flowers at some point throughout the night, and Calysta watched them flit around the crowd, impossible to miss. Novi had always been more social than most nymphs, seeming to open up and truly bloom the more they were with their kind.

Calysta sighed, falling back to stare up at the sky as her fingers played with the soft blades of grass. Petal-pink hair fanned around her, shining in the starlight. Alcohol buzzed in her veins, a feeling that made her miss the mercs. She'd lived without them for 165 years, but now that she knew them, had been a part of their little chosen family, she knew she'd always missed them ... always needed them.

The music slowly faded, not quite dying out, but becoming ambient background noise, and Calysta sat up, looking over to where most of the nymphs were gathered.

A water nymph, the dark blue of his skin only just discernible in the dim light, stood on a rock, hands raised as the crowd grew hushed. His slate-gray hair hung freely about his shoulders, and his pitch black eyes scanned the crowd. "Tonight we celebrate, knowing that our connection to Nethyl is our own. That it is inherent. That no one can take it from us. Tonight we celebrate, knowing that our rituals and our magic are our own, and we will be free to carry on the traditions of our past that have fed our world for hundreds of thousands of years." He smiled, dropping his arms and folding his hands over his chest.

"Tonight we celebrate the end of our current persecution. We celebrate the knowledge that we are able to take action against those who would wish to keep us under their thumbs. We celebrate the death of Illiziana Fielder."

A cacophony of cheers rose up from the gathered nymphs, but Calysta sat frozen to the ground, her mouth popped open. She knew that Illiziana had caused trouble for the nymphs and that having her out of the way would be seen as a blessing, but if they were claiming responsibility for her death ...

Worry, cold and heavy, curled its way through Calysta.

The nymphs had hired Aleah.

She felt stupid for not having pieced it together before. Who else would want the overseer gone? Why else would Novi suddenly need her to be back? Calysta was meant to witness something great, a dawn of new life for her folk. *We never deserved her persecution*, she thought. And while Calysta wasn't remorseful in the least that Illiziana was now dead, a different unease wormed through her, one she couldn't quite place.

The sweetness of the liquor grew sharp and sour on Calysta's tongue, and she pushed up, her legs unsteady beneath her as she tried to work through the possibilities.

Novi had jumped up next to the water nymph, chin lifted and shoulders set. "It's time for us to band together. Nymphs once had free run of this land, feeding our magic to it and replenishing our magic from it in turn. We can live freely again! Who among the fae can say that they hold a claim to Nethyl stronger than ours?"

Calysta's mouth dried up, and she remembered the way the ley lines below the surface had pulled at her magic, the rush in her head as she'd felt the planet and its life, everything rushing toward one central point.

The Gate.

She shook her head, watching her old friend preach to the others about blood rights and history. The nymphs had no use for the Gate; that's why they'd charged Orym with its keeping so long ago. The nymphs cared only about Nethyl itself—the land, the water, the life—the things their magic manipulated.

But she still felt uneasy, disquiet tightening in her stomach uncomfortably. Calysta folded her arms across her belly, where the fabric of her short, flowing dress covered three jagged, raised scars, left over from a vicious demon attack the year prior when Basta had been hunting for ways to take the Gate's power for his own.

The clearing felt suffocating as Calysta tried to think, and she stumbled back a few steps before turning and running for the wall of vines, using her magic to part a path as she slipped through. She broke out into the forest on the other side, falling to her knees as she breathed in the cool night air. The faint scent of salt from the sea a few klicks south was refreshing after the cloying smell of lush, flowering plants from the meadow.

Calysta sat with her back against a tree trunk, pulling her knees to her chest as she tried to think. Her loyalties felt entirely split. On one hand, she wanted to tell Merriam about everything that had happened. She felt that Mollian, as king and as a Keeper, should know how the nymphs felt. On the other, the nymphs weren't technically doing anything wrong. They would never harm Nethyl. Organizing the assassination of a politician widely known for stifling their culture was one thing. That was personal, Calysta decided, but going back to their roots and connecting to their world as they once had ... was there really any harm in that?

Was Novi right in thinking that Calysta had spent too much time around non-nymphs? Had she lost those wild little bits of herself that belonged to no one except for the planet whose magic gave her life?

Calysta sighed, drawing brambles up around her to protect her as she slept. It would do no one any good for her to be making these decisions while intoxicated. Best to sleep it off. *I can think on it more in the morning.*

The only thing Calysta was certain of, as sleep claimed her, was that she felt oddly in the middle, pulled by both her past and her present and unwilling to turn her back on either.

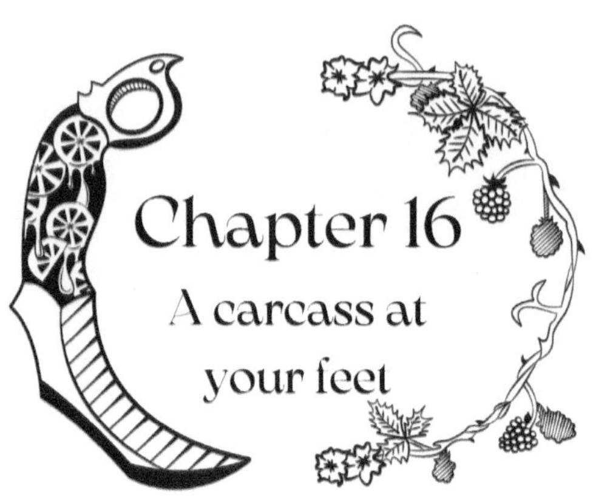

Chapter 16

A carcass at
your feet

THE JOURNEY HOME WENT way too quickly by Aleah's standards. As the city of Umbra appeared on the mountainside ahead of them, the readiness she felt to finally be home was waylaid by a pang of sadness that she would no longer be on the road with Kodi. He'd still had Guard responsibilities to take care of, but they were so minimal while traveling, and he was always close by. Even when they weren't together, they were almost always within each other's line of sight.

And line of sight typically led to one or the other gradually drifting over, both of them caught in the other's orbit.

Kodi was still very much riding the high of Aleah's proclamation of love. Hearing those words from her lips had awakened something in him that completely overshadowed whatever he'd previously felt. She was his overlord, and he would happily worship at her feet until his dying breath.

On that final day, he rode at the back of the caravan with the mercenaries, playing sight and word games with them and a few other guardsmen who also held the back line. The Royal Guard had many variations of these games, different detachments and groups coming up with different rules and evolutions of the same base. It helped the time go by, and most of them were entirely simple, but the specific rules were never shared, rather had to be figured out by each player as the game went on.

"I'm bringing, um … a knife," Kodi said, smiling smugly.

"I'm bringing, um … a jug of water," Jasper added.

Aleah glowered. She was the only one of the group who'd yet to figure out the rule. "I'm going scouting, and I'm bringing pikes to impale all of you."

A couple of the Guard looked unsure how to respond, but Kodi and Jasper burst into laughter.

"Sorry, Aleah, you can't bring pikes to impale all of us," Calysta told her sympathetically. "But I'll bring, um … pikes to impale all of us." She grinned, and Aleah threw her hands up in frustration.

"I'll bring, um … a shovel, so Aleah can bury our bodies after," one of the Guard said, a smile playing on her lips, unsure whether or not she was allowed in on the joke.

Kodi snorted so hard he almost choked, clutching his stomach as he doubled over.

Despite her frustration, Aleah joined in the laughter. "No need, Lexi, I'll be leaving you all up to rot."

"We're almost home. Give it another go, Aleah," Kodi prompted, wiping tears from beneath his eyes. "What are you bringing scouting?"

She fiddled with the reins in her hands, trying to figure out what it was she was missing. "I'm bringing …" She flicked her gaze over to Kodi, who was watching her expectantly.

"Come on, little merc, you've got this," he encouraged.

Aleah pursed her lips against a smile, turning her eyes up to the sky. "I'm bringing, um … a pardon from the Crown for murdering you all."

A collective whoop went up from their little group, causing some people further ahead to turn and give them curious or concerned looks.

"You can bring your pardon," Kodi confirmed.

"*What?*" Aleah squeaked, crossing her arms over her chest. "I can bring a pardon, but not anything else?"

"No, you can also bring a bedroll, remember? You got that, too," Calysta reminded her.

Aleah looked pleadingly at Kodi. "What is it? What's the rule?"

He shrugged. "The rule is that no one is allowed to tell you the rule—you've got to figure it out on your own."

"Think about what you said, Aleah. You're overcomplicating it," Jasper offered.

She huffed, pinning him with an unamused look. "I'll overcomplicate something for you," she grumbled.

"Let me know when you've decided what that means, so I can take the threat seriously," he teased.

Then, all too quickly, they were in the city, the mercenaries splitting off to head home. They dismounted at the side of the street, unstrapping their belongings from the horses.

Kodi also slid down to the ground, helping Aleah with the strap from her pack, which she stood on tiptoe trying to reach. She hooked it over her shoulder, and he pulled her close to his chest, pressing his face to the top of her head. Her bright hair was warm from the sunshine, and the smell of her sent him back to picking wild fruit from the vine. "I'll see you soon."

Aleah tipped her face up, nipping at his throat. "And then you'll tell me the rule?"

"You own me, Aleah." He lowered his face to kiss her. "But not a chance." He tossed a parting smile and salute to Jasper and Calysta before hooking leads to their horses, which were from the royal stables, and returning to his mount.

Aleah watched him go with a sigh before following her friends into the alley behind their home. "I don't suppose either of you can be bribed to share?"

"Sorry, red. We're in surprisingly good relations with the Guard at the moment, and I'm not going to be the one to ruin it," Jasper said, and Calysta laughed.

Aleah was about to argue, but as soon as they walked through the door of the merc house, she smelled something baking, and her mouth instantly watered. She dropped her pack in the hallway and skipped into the kitchen, sliding to a stop behind Campbell and wrapping her arms around his middle. "Have I ever told you you're my favorite?" she asked.

Campbell smiled, leaning into her and looking over as Jasper and Calysta walked in. "Did you two do something, or is it just the cake I've got in the oven?"

"A mix of both, probably," Calysta answered.

Aleah released Campbell, hopping up to sit on the counter and pulling a mixing bowl from the sink. "Is Leo in town?" She wiped a finger along the side of the bowl and popped it into her mouth.

"Yeah, he's just at the aviary today. Horscha ended up taking a few days off." Campbell stirred the caramel sauce on the stovetop in front of him. "How was the job?"

"Officially, everything went off without a hitch," Jasper said, coming into the kitchen to grab a glass of water.

"Unofficially," Calysta added, folding her arms and leaning against the doorframe. "We've got a feral Ranger on our hands."

"Is this a Merriam problem or an Aleah problem?" Campbell asked, removing the pot from the heat.

"It's not a problem at all." Aleah scooped more batter from the bowl. "Well, yet. We'll cross that bridge if we come to it, I suppose."

"*When* we come to it," Jasper corrected.

Aleah grinned, despite the potential consequences of either murder. "Jasper added kidnapping to his resume."

Campbell turned to look at him in shocked surprise. "Who'd you kidnap?"

"Her uncle," Jasper said. "Kodi was the mastermind behind it, though."

"You're not going to make me wait for Leo to get home before telling me about this, are you?"

Aleah happily obliged, allowing Jasper and Calysta to go unpack and shower, while she told Campbell everything she knew about what had happened with Chetney.

Campbell removed the cake from the oven as he listened, setting it aside to cool and resting a hip against the counter across from Aleah. "The scar replication is oddly romantic."

"Yeah," Aleah sighed dreamily, holding the now-empty bowl in her lap. "I told him I love him," she admitted, a blush crawling up her freckled cheeks.

"Do you want him to go around killing everyone who's ever wronged you? Because that's probably a great way to reach that goal."

"Oh, like Leonidas wouldn't run a sword through any of those assholes you used to run with before I found you," Aleah shot back.

Campbell scratched the base of an antler, giving a sheepish frown of acquiescence. "He really does have a thing about people putting their hands on me, doesn't he?"

"That protective streak runs long and deep," Aleah agreed.

Early the morning after they returned home, the hinges on Aleah's window creaked softly as it swung open. Something dropped to the floor, followed by the quiet scuffle of footsteps in a gait entirely familiar to her.

"Who dares disturb my slumber?" she grumbled.

A slight weight settled on the mattress next to her. "A male whose love for you borders on obsession."

Aleah was entirely unprepared for the way her stomach tumbled with the words, and she rolled over, biting against a smile and blinking sleep from her eyes. Kodi knelt by her bed, arms folded on the edge and chin resting on them as he watched her. She reached out, pushing her fingers into his golden brown mohawk, and his eyes fluttered closed with her touch. "Obsession, huh?"

His gaze found hers, green and blue soft with serenity. "It's a very welcome intrusion."

"Better, now that you're allowed to tell me?" she teased, but her chest tightened at the way he looked at her, and she couldn't even pretend like her entire body wasn't now a live wire, waiting for his touch.

He tipped his head up, causing her hand to slide to his cheek so that he could nuzzle her palm. "I should have tried dropping a carcass at your feet ages ago."

"A carcass?" she questioned with a laugh.

"That's what you call dead animals." He gave a noncommittal shrug.

She tugged the sleeve of his shirt, all the prompting he needed to crawl into bed next to her. She snuggled against him, kissing his neck before pinching the skin lightly between her teeth. "Move in with me."

"Okay." The simplicity of his answer was undermined by his elevated heart rate, his pulse thrumming wildly as he slipped a hand into Aleah's hair.

She pulled back to look at him. "Can you, really?"

"Of course. I'm a Ranger, not a prisoner."

"It's that easy, then?" she asked, a slow smile spreading over her face. She shifted closer, dragging her nails down his neck.

He shuddered, his hand going to her hip, thumb drawing circles over her skin where her shirt had ridden up in sleep. "There's a housing form to fill out for official purposes, but yes. Once you've been in the Guard over five years, it's that easy."

"I'll talk to the others about it today." Aleah licked his throat before biting him and hooking her leg over his.

Kodi hissed, squeezing her hip over a mostly healed bruise, and pulled her closer. "When will I know whether or not I've been voted in?" He rolled, pinning her beneath him.

"They know better than to deny me this," her confident words melded into a whimper as he slid down, dropping his mouth to her cunt over the thin cotton of her sleep shorts.

A rumbling sound of desire came from his chest, and then they were tearing off each other's clothes, and Kodi was back between her legs. "Safeword," he demanded.

"Carcass," she answered, breathless with desire and anticipation.

There was absolutely nothing teasing about Kodi's movements. His lips, tongue, and teeth worked over her clit in every way he knew drove her crazy, and as her legs clamped on either side of his head and her hand fisted in his hair, he pushed his fingers inside of her, giving her fluttering walls something to clench around.

Her free hand reached for his shoulder, scratching as she arched her back and gasped for breath. "Kodi, Kodi, wait. Don't, you're gonna make me—*fuck*, Kodi." Her first orgasm came on fast and strong, waves of pleasure knocking through her body as she cried out.

He took his time with the subsequent ones, both of them sweaty and panting by the time they were finished. Kodi rolled off of her, one arm tucked under his head. Shifting to her side to face him and propping herself up on an elbow, Aleah drew her finger around the bruises on his bicep, each one tipped with a small crescent shape where her nails had dug into his skin.

"Admiring your handiwork?" he asked wryly, turning his head to bite at her fingers.

She let his teeth close around one and smiled, trying to ignore the way her stomach flipped. "Is it okay that loving you is the most terrifying thing that's ever happened to me?"

Kodi reached over to brush away a lock of hair that stuck to her brow. "It's only fitting, since loving you also terrifies me."

"Does it?"

"You spark something feral in me, Aleah. I mean it when I say there is not much in this world I wouldn't trade my right arm to give you."

She pouted playfully. "What about your left?"

"That one is much more adept at both wielding a knife and drawing the most deliciously filthy words from your mouth. The left, I keep." Kodi leaned in to kiss her before pushing up from the bed. "Shower?" He held out the aforementioned left hand.

By the time they were clean and decent, the rest of the house had woken up, and the sound of voices drifted from the mushroom as they walked downstairs.

"Fancy seeing you here, Ranger," Calysta said from where she sprawled across the couch, lazily popping cherries into her mouth.

"There's sausage and eggs in the kitchen," Campbell offered, wiping grease from his mouth with the back of his hand. He sat on the floor in front of Leonidas, the blonde's legs on either side of him.

Leonidas had a clipboard in his lap, his brow furrowed as he flipped one page back and forth, trying to make something add up. He glanced up as Kodi walked into the room, Aleah having disappeared to grab them food. "Are you heading back up to the castle soon?"

"I'm on rest and recoup from the Do Lech trip, so I'm not on a schedule today."

Leonidas sighed, running a hand over his short-cropped hair. "Horscha is out of town, so I'll be busy all day, but your guys at the castle aviary have either done their paperwork wrong or about seven ravens have appeared out of thin air. Do you mind dropping this off on your way home? I've marked where the inconsistencies seem to be, so they should be able to figure it out."

"Speaking of home," Aleah interrupted, waltzing in with a loaded plate. "I asked Kodi to move in." She plopped down next to him, handing him the plate and plucking two muffins and a link of sausage from the top.

A smile pulled at Jasper's mouth, but he didn't look up from the sock he was darning. "Any objections?" he asked. The others looked at each other, something happy and knowing in all their faces. "I think we've all been waiting for the day you would officially become an honorary merc. Welcome home." Jasper turned his smile on Kodi then, approval and camaraderie bright in his silver eyes.

Kodi was taken aback by the warmth and belonging that filled his chest because of the people around him. He had the Rangers, and that brotherhood was something he'd never taken for granted. But this was a different kind of acceptance, one based on affinity rather than a rite of passage, and he was equally proud to be part of this circle—this family.

Chapter 17

Mer's in trouble

THE DAY AFTER ALEAH invited Kodi to move in, a raven flew through the office window, letting out a loud croak that woke Panic from a dead sleep. He was so startled that he immediately launched himself at the corvid with a piercing *scree*, knocking it to the floor. Leonidas called him off with a sharp whistle, and Panic hopped back, glaring at the other, now equally startled, bird and clicking his beak in complaint.

Leonidas recognized the brass circlet around the bird's ankle and pulled the tiny scroll attached to it. "Did those nincompoops finally figure out how to properly log their incoming birds?" he asked, picking up the raven and placing him on a perch. He fished around in one of the desk drawers for a treat and fed it to the raven, Panic hopping closer with a soft rustle of feathers and tilting his head innocently.

"You just attacked him for no reason," Leonidas said.

Panic chirped before hopping up next to the raven, who scooted to the very edge of the perch, and blinked at Leonidas.

He sighed. "You're incorrigible." But he tossed a treat to the falcon regardless and sank down into the desk chair to read the note.

Immediately, he was back on his feet, running out into the hall. "Jasper!" he called.

"Mushroom!" The answer floated up to him, and he dropped down the stairs two at a time.

"Mer's in trouble," he said before he'd reached the main floor.

"What kind of trouble?" Jasper asked.

Leonidas held up the note. "No one has seen her since last night. Mollian hasn't *felt* her since last night."

Aleah was tucked into a corner of the couch, sitting cross-legged with Campbell across from her. The playing cards she held in her hand dropped as her grip loosened, the color draining from her face. Her breathing grew shallow, blood rushing loudly in her ears, and every single scar her uncle had given her flared to life with the memory of why she'd been given them. His *mehhen* was dead, and Aleah was not.

Her vision tunneled, a whimper at the ghost of pain across her body clawing its way up her throat. Merriam was gone, and Mollian was so very powerful. Warm hands with long, nimble fingers squeezed hers, and she blinked, meeting Campbell's steady indigo gaze. She swallowed back her terror, ignoring the way her shirt brushed against her scars. Merriam, her friend—her sister—needed her. She swung her legs from the couch, still gripping one of Campbell's hands.

Jasper caught her gaze, those intelligent silver eyes reading her resolve as he stood. "Let's go." Like a choreographed dance, the mercenaries moved, donning shoes and weapons in grim silence, energy crackling between them as they quickly moved out onto the street, racing up to the castle.

One of their own was in danger, and they wouldn't rest until they brought her home.

Aleah's heart pounded a steady rhythm as they neared the castle gates. The guardsmen standing watch had been told to expect them, directing them to the war room. Fear still swirled sickeningly through her belly, but resolve kept her moving forward, steeling her mind against the way it threatened to plummet into oblivion.

Her resolve held strong until she walked into the war room. She'd barely had a chance to glance at Mollian and mark the agitated set of his shoulders and the wild energy seeping from him before Rovin had met her eyes, and she thought she might vomit.

She was shaking her head almost before he'd even spoken. *Not Kodi.* She needed to be here, would do whatever she could to help Merriam, but she couldn't put Kodi in Mollian's path if the worst happened. If something happened to him ... she swallowed hard.

"Please, I wouldn't ask if it wasn't vital," Rovin pleaded, holding her gaze. And it was that shimmer of anguished worry in his brown eyes that made her feet move almost of their own volition, back through the castle and out into the courtyard. Her steps felt rhythmic as she climbed the stone steps of the outer walls, moving to the parapets where she knew Kodi was on duty.

He was moving down the wide walkway as soon as he saw her, reading her body language in the moonlight before she was close enough to fully see her face. "What's wrong?" he asked, stopping in front of her and reaching for her hands as he searched her face.

"Rovin needs you," she said, her voice wavering. "Mer's gone."

Kodi's eyes widened, a flurry of emotions crossing his face as he processed everything, understanding immediately what those two words meant to Aleah. He turned his head to call over his shoulder. "Hold it down up here for a bit, yeah?"

He waited only long enough for the other Ranger to give a salute of acknowledgement before taking Aleah's hand and moving at a brisk pace back down to the castle. "What happened?" he asked as they walked.

Aleah swallowed past the lump in her throat, Kodi's calloused palm against hers incredibly grounding. "Nobody's seen her since yesterday, not even Molli."

"Shit," he breathed, pulling her toward the barracks. "Wait here." He dipped inside, quickly returning with an extra sword strapped around his waist. "Something tells me our gallant lover-boy might not have been adequately armed when he ran off in search of the demonslayer earlier." He flashed Aleah a reassuring grin, pulling her closer. "Don't you worry about me, little merc."

She swallowed against her terror, leaning into him as they hurried toward the war room.

Chapter 18
A different Guard

MERRIAM HAD BEEN RESCUED, and Ferrick was dead. After seeing what Kodi had done to Chetney, Aleah had been positive that there was no way a person could be *more* dead than her uncle had been. Then she'd seen the hundreds of chunks of flesh and bone that Ferrick had been reduced to and known she was wrong.

That was as dead as dead could get.

Once they'd returned to Umbra and taken Merriam to see a medic, Aleah stayed with her through the night and most of the morning. Mollian had slipped away for only a couple of hours to deal with establishing and vetting a temporary control of the Guard, including ensuring Eskar was kept under constant watch until they could get more information from her. He hadn't been able to stay away from Merriam for long, though, and had soon returned.

Much like Merriam, Aleah had never been good at nor fond of helping people sift through their emotions, but the stiff set of Mollian's shoulders and the pained pinch of his eyebrows were too much for her to bear, so she'd sat with him while he worked with his tools. She pestered him with questions about designs for different weapons, played with the various garnishings, and did her best to keep his mind from slipping back to all the what-ifs that hadn't transpired and to keep him from trying to punish himself for things that were out of his control.

And then there was Merriam, whose avoidant tendencies matched Aleah's. While in captivity, Eskar convinced her that Rovin had betrayed her, but Aleah knew better than to try to push her friend into talking about it or dealing with it before she was ready.

So, after a phenomenal breakfast in the king's quarters, Aleah parted ways with Merriam in the courtyard to go see Kodi before she went home. A lot would be changing in his world in the next few days, and now that Merriam was at least settled and safe, she needed to check on him.

A guardsman was posted outside of the door, shaking his head as she walked up. "Entry is restricted to Rangers only."

Her brow furrowed. "Since when?" Then she folded her arms across her chest, exasperated both with herself and with the Ranger in front of her. Of course, everyone was being kept under close watch until the rest of Ferrick's supporters were found. "I just want to see Kodi. Can you tell him I'm here?"

"Sorry, merc. I can't leave my post."

"You don't need to leave. Just poke your head inside and get someone's attention!" Aleah took a calming breath, forcing her volume lower. "Look, I understand—"

"Is there a problem?" a strong, confident voice interrupted.

The Ranger snapped to attention. "No, sir, I was just informing the mercenary she's not permitted inside the barracks."

Aleah whirled around, meeting the piercing blue gaze of Commander Dio. His golden hair gleamed in the early afternoon sun, every strand perfectly in place. She wet her lips, preparing to plead her case to the fae she'd challenged across the table in the war room what felt like a lifetime ago.

Dio broke her stare, looking at the Ranger over her shoulder. "Thank you, Garret. I'll keep an eye on her."

Aleah's mouth popped open, but she quickly wiped the surprise from her face and followed Dio into the barracks.

"There's going to be a lot happening while we figure out how to move forward after Ferrick's treason," he told her quietly, his voice almost drowned out by the din of multiple conversations taking place at once. "There's a short list of people Mollian trusts right now, and they're going to be busiest while we work through this." He looked down at Aleah, and the softness in his expression shocked her enough to root her feet to the floor. "The Guard will need Kodi during this transition, but I know a lot happened last night, so go see him."

She blinked, taken aback by his transparency and the way he talked to her like they were on an even level. It wasn't something she was used to from the higher ranking Guard. "Thank you," she said with a tentative smile, giving him a last, appreciative nod before weaving through the various groups of Rangers to where she spied Kodi leaning against the wall.

He straightened when he saw her, surprised delight bright on his face. "How'd you weasel your way in here?" he asked as she slid into his side, wrapping her arms around his waist as his went around her shoulders.

"Commander Dio escorted me himself, actually, no weaseling involved." She grinned up at him.

"So Kodi gets a girl during lockdown, but the rest of us have to do without?" one of the Rangers in their small circle joked.

Kodi just cocked an eyebrow, looking over Aleah's head and lifting a middle finger.

"You need a girl first before worrying about whether or not she's allowed to visit, Percy," another cut in.

Aleah laughed, turning to face the others. "You'll need to stop being such a twat before you expect to get a girl," she added.

Percy slapped his chest, stumbling back a few steps in the pretense of being wounded.

Kodi rolled his eyes, brushing his thumb over Aleah's arm to pull her attention back before moving a few steps away from the group. "How is she?" he asked softly, and Aleah melted at the concern in his eyes.

"She's okay. Refuses to be kept under watch, which I guess shouldn't surprise any of us." Aleah gave him a wry smile. "I'd ask you to keep an eye out for her, but she'd gut me if she knew I made the request."

"And you know I will anyway," Kodi said with an easy shrug. "Though I doubt Mollian's going to give anyone the chance to try anything. If anyone knew how Ferrick died ..."

"They don't?" Aleah asked. Clearly the Guard had been told about the treason, but she was unsure how many details had been shared.

Kodi shook his head, scanning the room with an agitated set to his shoulders. "The official brief was that Ferrick made a move against

Merriam and the Crown, and Mollian killed him for it. No one has been told specifics. Right now, we're just waiting to figure out who else might have been in on it or might support Ferrick's actions."

Aleah followed his gaze across the room, suppressing a shiver that some of these people would align with Ferrick's classist, extremist ideals. Then she suddenly remembered Merriam's refusal to come to the barracks with her and lifted onto her tiptoes as she again surveyed the crowd. "Where's Rovin?"

"He was with Bellamy the last I saw him. They're sort of ... heading the investigation with Commander Dio. It's a very temporary chain of command and tenuous at that, but Mollian was understandably on edge about who he can actually trust when he put the Guard on lockdown last night."

"And Rovin Arwood made that cut." Aleah laughed with a quiet wonder, then her smile fell, her brows pulling together in a frown. "How is he?"

Kodi sighed, leaning heavily against the wall and pushing a hand into his curls. "He's hurt, but he doesn't blame her. He knows that it's the part he played in the past that allowed Mer to believe those accusations in the first place." He swallowed, looking at the space between their feet as he dropped his hand to grab Aleah's. "I played a part in that past, too."

"Ko," she said softly, waiting for him to meet her eyes. "She forgave you for all of that a long time ago. You know that."

He blinked against the tears lining his eyes, dropping her gaze. "But what happened to her—"

"Had nothing to do with you or Rovin," Aleah cut in, searching his face. "Tell me you know that, because if you try to take the blame for what that sick fuck did, I'm going to have to kick your ass in front of every Ranger here."

A mirthless chuckle bubbled from Kodi's chest, and he tucked Aleah against him, closing his eyes as he held her. "We're gonna get through this. All of us." His fingers curled over the tip of her clipped ear, and he squeezed her tighter. "This is going to be a different Guard. I'll make sure of it."

Kodi's heart thumped a steady rhythm beneath Aleah's cheek, each beat accompanied within her by a flaring pulse of untamed possession. It wasn't even just how much she claimed him, but an understanding that she belonged to him in turn. And the recognition of that didn't scare her—didn't make her want to push him away and run. Instead, she tipped her head back to look at him, searching the raw emotion in his face. Contrition, but also a fierce determination. She understood then everything that the Guard truly meant to him and the pride that came with his title of Ranger. She loved this part of him, still wild, but driven, given a purpose. It looked so good on him that she could have melted. "You're *mine*, Kodi, but they need you here. More than I do, for once." A smile twitched at her lips. "Fix your Guard."

He held his face in her hands and pressed a kiss to her forehead. "After all of this is taken care of, once we've rooted out the rest of Ferrick's insurrection and Mollian has sworn in a new captain, I'll be waking up in your bed every morning. And I cannot fucking wait."

Chapter 19

Dance with me?

ALMOST A FORTNIGHT AFTER Merriam was taken, Leonidas ate a late breakfast in the kitchen of the merc house, leaning a hip against the counter as he speared eggs with a fork. He'd woken up early to make the rounds at the aviary, ensuring all of the birds were taken care of before locking up for the full moons festival, which Horscha also had the day off for.

A knock sounded on the back door just as Campbell was walking down the stairs, hair damp from a shower. "Impeccable timing." He went down the hall, and moments later, the patter of little boots filled the air as Ryddan came running into the house.

"Paaaaaaan!" The prince shifted into a wolf as he rounded the corner, and the falcon dove from his perch with an equally loud screech, barreling into him. Ryddan fell dramatically to his side, then jumped up, his rump wiggling in the air before he lept at Panic.

"Hey, don't roughhouse in the mushroom," Bellamy reprimanded, following Campbell into the room.

Ryddan shifted back into his fae form, legs splayed in front of him where he sat on the floor. His big, green eyes looked at Bellamy first, then moved to Campbell. "Sorry," he said abashedly.

Panic stood between Ryddan's feet, looking up at Bellamy accusingly for having halted their game.

Leonidas snapped his fingers, pulling the falcon's attention. He cocked an eyebrow at him. "If you keep getting him in trouble, he's going to stop visiting you. Behave yourself." He pointed his fork to punctuate his point, and Panic glided over, hoping for a bite of egg.

Ryddan hopped up, too, walking over to give Campbell a hug before moving to Leonidas. "Why are you eating eggs?" he asked, arms wrapping around one of the man's legs.

Setting his plate on the counter, Leonidas smoothed a hand over Ryddan's hair, then leaned down to pick him up, settling him on one hip. "You don't eat eggs for breakfast?" he asked, scooping up another mouthful.

Ryddan scrunched his nose up. "Well, yeah, but it's the full moons festival today. Wouldn't you rather have a candy apple?"

Leonidas gave him an incredulous look. "Boy, you are out of your Legends-damned mind if you don't think I'm having a candy apple later. But I'm a lot bigger than you and need a little protein to tide me over."

"Leo needs to feed his muscles or he gets grumpy," Aleah chimed in as she came down the stairs. She scratched Ryddan's back as she slid by to head into the kitchen.

Ryddan pushed down from Leonidas as Aleah pulled a jug of milk from the ice box, resting his hands on the counter and watching as she poured a glass.

Without questioning, she patted the counter and pulled a second glass from the cupboard. Ryddan clambered up, sitting down with his feet dangling over the edge, while Aleah pulled out a container of powdered chocolate to mix into his glass.

"It's starting to make sense why he wants to come with Mer every time she visits," Bellamy said, watching as Ryddan roped Aleah into a very intense conversation about swamp animals while they drank.

Campbell dropped to the couch to pull on his boots. "You should see the mess he and Aleah make when they try to bake together. I swear more flour ends up on them than in the recipe."

"It's impressive how she manages to turn clean up into a game, though. That's a skill I didn't even know existed," Leonidas said, then caught the question on Bellamy's face before he could voice it. "Not a method Lydia would probably condone, much less implement."

Campbell snorted. "I don't think there's a single thing about Aleah that Lydia would condone. Speaking of ..." He cut a glance at Bellamy, a mischievous grin spreading across his face. The night they'd rescued Merriam, Leonidas and Campbell had stayed with Bellamy to protect Ryddan, and Lydia had been hanging off the Ranger with the biggest doe eyes any of them had ever seen.

Bellamy groaned, rolling his eyes. "What are the odds she'll leave me alone today?"

"Today? During Sekha's largest celebration of the year?" Leonidas slung a tattooed arm over Bellamy's shoulders. "I hope you're planning to join the sparring tourneys, because Cam and I have bets on how often she'll take her eyes off of you. And if you end up covered in sweat and showing off your muscles, I'm set to earn a pretty bit of coin."

But any bets about the nursemaid's unrequited longing were forgotten once the sun began to dip below the mountains in the west and Rovin showed up to accompany Merriam.

Leonidas thought he'd done a good job of covering his surprise, but as they walked to the amphitheater to watch one of the first productions of the night, he couldn't stop turning it over in his head, wondering when he'd missed signs of something developing between them.

"You can't really be that daft, Leo," Aleah laughed as they took their seats.

"Ever since you and Kodi got together, she's hardly gone a day without complaining about how much she has to be around Rovin and how he's so insufferable and—" Leonidas stopped, resisting the urge to slap a hand to his face and instead turning to look where Merriam sat between Mollian and Rovin, a slight flush to her cheeks and a gleam of happiness in her eyes. "Okay, yup. I'm as blind as a mole rat without its whiskers."

"You've been planning this," Campbell accused, folding his arms over his chest. "And you didn't even tell me?"

Jasper reached over to muss his curls. "You'd have done nothing but tried to tease her about it, and then she'd have dug her heels in and run the opposite direction."

"But *you* knew?" Campbell raised a suspicious brow.

"It's not my fault neither of you were observant enough to watch whenever Aleah *oh-so-casually* planned nights out in tandem with the Rangers. Mer went beet red almost every time he talked to her." Jasper shrugged.

"Drunk Mer is horrible at masking emotions," Aleah sighed happily, leaning her head against Kodi's shoulder and focusing her attention to the front as actors filed across the stage, ready to begin.

After the show, under the brilliant light of the twin full moons, was the sparring tournament. While Leonidas had been interested in trying his skills against a guardsman or two, he was aware of Campbell's head cocked towards the music that floated from across the meadow and his feet tapping a matching rhythm against the wooden bleachers.

Panic grew agitated with the noise and compression of the crowds, so Leonidas sent him home before leading Campbell into the rows of stalls, meandering toward the music. He had an arm draped over Campbell's shoulders, the other holding a cup of mead. Many vendors sold various wares and treats, and the two stopped briefly to glance at the things for sale as they moved through the crowd, sipping their drinks.

Campbell's fingers drummed against Leonidas' hand as they moved closer to the sound of the music. Finishing his mead, Leonidas reached over to guide Campbell's mug to his mouth to encourage the same before taking both cups and leaving them on one of the tables set out to collect used dishes. "Dance with me?" he asked, palm held out.

Campbell's answering grin was brighter than the moons as he took the offered hand and led Leonidas into the throng of people dancing in front of a raised stage where a band was playing lively music.

Leonidas knew how to move his feet in a fight, understood his build, and how to be fluid and light in battle. He did not, however, understand how to move to the rhythm of music in any graceful manner.

But Campbell did, and his enjoyment of it was more than enough to chase away any sense of self-consciousness Leonidas might have felt. They danced together, Campbell spinning circles around Leonidas, his hips and feet matching the beat of the music and arms thrown up into the air without a care in the world.

After a few songs, a familiar measure played that signaled the start of a group dance, and Leonidas brushed a quick kiss to Campbell's temple before bowing out. He stopped at a nearby vendor for some food and stood at the edge of the crowd, watching as Campbell danced with the others around him, spinning, clapping, and stomping their feet. Campbell looked over his shoulder, indigo meeting ice-blue with a gleeful glimmer, and added an extra, seductively confident swivel of his hips before his attention snapped back to the dance.

When the song ended, Campbell skipped over to Leonidas, who leaned down to kiss him. "How are you so damned sexy?"

Campbell brushed away the curls stuck to his forehead with a cocky smile, reaching to take the turkey leg Leonidas held in one hand. "It's the antlers." He winked as he tore a strip of meat free and popped it into his mouth. Ripping off another chunk of meat, he glanced around the clearing before remembering that Panic had gone back to the merc house, and his smile dropped for a moment.

Leonidas looped an arm around Campbell's shoulders, pulling him close to press his lips to the top of his head as his entire heart melted. "Legends, I love you."

"I love you, too." Campbell tipped his face up for a kiss, his smile back in full brilliance as he linked an arm with Leonidas'. "Come on, let's go look at the art displays. I could use another drink, too."

While waiting in line for mead, they spotted Bellamy walking through the crowd and waved him over. "Rydd with Lydia?" Campbell asked.

Bellamy joined them in line, tucking his hands into his pockets. "I love that kid too much to let her fuss at him all night," he joked. "The captain is actually watching him for a bit."

"Dio's girls are feral little creatures," Leonidas remarked fondly.

"They're wild, but they both *love* the Crown's hunting hawks," Campbell interpreted for Bellamy, digging into his pocket for a few coppers to exchange for three cups of mead. "We were headed over to the arts grove if you wanted to come."

"Actually, there's a performance I was planning to watch. Magic stuff." Bellamy accepted the cup Campbell held to him. "Thanks."

The antlered male waved him off as they moved from the line, taking a deep pull.

Leonidas looked at Bellamy, one eyebrow raised skeptically. "Magic?"

"Not normal magic, tricks and jokes with cards and coins," the Ranger explained, maneuvering carefully through the throngs of people. "Mer met Shiloh in Do Lech, and I've never seen anything like what they do. They're fair folk, too, so no glamors or anything! You've got to see it."

"I'm game for tricks," Campbell said, and they followed Bellamy to a corner of the tents where a decent crowd was already lingering.

A leather-clad fae was seated on a wide stump, legs crossed in front of them, and four slender, translucent wings draped down their back, sparkling in the moonlight. Their arms were covered in fine lines of black ink, some flowers, some geometric, and a flash of what looked like a skull on the underside of a forearm. Shiloh glanced over the front of the crowd, holding eye contact with three people and pointing to them in turn. "You keep your eyes on the cups, okay? You're covering the best angles, so if you see any funny business, it's up to you three to call me out."

Shiloh held a small ball between their thumb and forefinger, giving it a good squeeze to show its resistance before placing it underneath one of the three wooden cups in front of them. "Don't lose the ball," they said, flashing a cheeky grin before sliding the cups around, slowly at first, but picking up speed. Then they lifted their hands in the air, pointing to one of the people they'd singled out before. "Which cup, my friend?"

"The middle!"

Shiloh looked to the other two. "Do you both agree?" They nodded, and Shiloh lifted the middle cup to reveal ... nothing. "Another guess, then?" they asked the whole crowd, and there were an equal amount of shouts for left and right. Shiloh lifted one, then the other, but the ball was nowhere to be found. They stacked the cups on top of each other, then set them back out. This time, when they lifted the middle, the ball was there. People clapped, and Shiloh rolled smoothly into the rest of their performance.

Campbell was just as enraptured as Bellamy, but in a different way. His thief's fingers itched to know how the fae was able to move objects with such unbelievable dexterity. Some simple things, like most of the coin tricks, he had perfected long ago, but to make something with more bulk seemingly disappear was a talent he felt desperate to learn.

"Come on, buck, you can accost them after the festival," Leonidas teased after the show, Campbell's indigo eyes dark in the moonlight, but that hungry gleam for knowledge more than readable. "Arts, remember?"

"Yeah," Campbell sighed, turning away. "Arts."

Bellamy went with them, browsing the tents of paintings, sculptures, rugs, jewelry, and all manner of beautiful things both practical and impractical that citizens around Jekeida had created. Campbell was debating the purchase of a set of kitchen knives, the block and handles carved with different kinds of mushrooms, when Aleah and Kodi found them, Jasper in tow and looking decidedly drunk.

"It's the full moons festival, Cam." Aleah sidled up behind him, wrapping her arms around his middle and peering around him. "Every indulgence is justified!"

Jasper pretended not to lose his balance, his wings starting to flare before he tucked them against his back and leaned his shoulder against a tent pole. "Yeah, every indulgence." He casually crossed one foot over the other.

Leonidas didn't even bother trying to hide his laughter, clapping Jasper on the shoulder. "Let's hope Calysta comes home from her ritual tomorrow prepared with a hangover cure."

"Silly Leo, she stocked us up before she went out." Aleah left Campbell to pay for his purchase, looking over the shiny, colorful wares stacked on the next table.

"I'm going to go check in with Captain Dio, make sure he's okay with Rydd. Then I should find Mollian in case he also needs rescuing," Bellamy said. "I'll see you all later."

They all said their goodbyes. Campbell cradled the knife set, now wrapped in paper, to his chest as they left the arts area.

"Anyone up for dancing?" Aleah asked.

Campbell nodded eagerly, looking at Leonidas.

"I'll walk Jaz home. Looks like he's had enough revelry for the night." Leonidas gripped Jasper's arm as the male swayed again.

Jasper shrugged with a sloppy grin. "Lord of Revelry's my surname, y'know."

"Kodi dubbed him earlier after he drank three guardsmen under the fucking table," Aleah explained with a laugh.

Leonidas shook his head, smiling as he took the knives from Campbell, leaning down to kiss him. "Be safe, okay? Enjoy the rest of the night."

"We will!" Aleah cut in, linking an arm through Campbell's. "Take care of our fearless leader, dear falconer." Then she looped her other arm through Kodi's and pulled them off into the crowd.

Jasper watched them go, his silver eyes bright in the moonlight. "She's so grown now. When did that happen? Feels like yesterday she was this tiny, savage thing. And now she's grown, taking her own jobs, falling in love ..."

"And still just as savage as ever." Leonidas knocked his shoulder into Jasper's. "Come on, you big sap. Let's get you home before you start trying to tell everyone how proud of them you are."

"I am, though," Jasper said as they walked towards Umbra. "Proud of you all. I never expected to have a family like this—so much comfort and love and talent all in one place."

"Talent for breaking the rules," Leonidas joked.

"Rules're arbitrary," Jasper slurred with a scoff.

Leonidas laughed again, thoroughly enjoying Jasper's inebriation. "I'm sure they are, Lord of Revelry."

Chapter 20

Nethyl calls to us

Calysta walked through the forest surrounding Umbra, dappled sunlight warming her skin as she moved between the trees. Citizens would gather from all over Jekeida for the full moons festival, a time full of merriment and revelry.

Calysta would not be attending.

Nervous anticipation swirled through her blood as she wandered along the edge of the massive clearing that bordered one side of Umbra, where tents and stalls had been set up days in advance to prepare for the festivities. But Calysta would be participating in something entirely different.

Illiziana Fielder was dead, thanks to Aleah, and hadn't had the chance to renew her legislation meant to hinder the ritual gatherings of the nymphs. For the first time in over one hundred years, her people would be free to gather together under the light of the full moons and give their magic back to the planet that gave them life.

She was beyond excited to participate in the rite, to celebrate Nethyl and her connection to its magic, but that excitement was edged with trepidation. Calysta understood better than most that the energy that gave Nethyl its magic and life was the same energy that fueled every reality in existence. The nymphs knew that the magic came from the Gate, but they never thought any deeper than that. Calysta had been to Entumbra, though, and had even visited Earth with Merriam a time or two. She couldn't help but wonder whether a flare of magic in her world would be mirrored in others.

With one firm, decided shake of her hands, Calysta flicked her worries away as if they were drops of water. Nymphs had been performing these rites for thousands and thousands of years before Illiziana had put a stop to them. Her people deserved this celebration—*she* deserved this celebration.

So she followed the pull of the ley line to the clearing where nymphs from around Jekeida had already begun to gather, drinking fruity wines and dancing, singing wild melodies as plants and water twirled through the air together.

Calysta joined them, happily accepting a horn of blackberry wine from a water nymph and tipping it back as the nymph pulled her into the circle. Some of the wine spilled down her chin, and she wiped the back of her hand across her mouth as she handed the horn back.

The nymphs lost themselves in revelry until the sun set and the moons rose high overhead, filling the clearing with their silvery light. Then the mushrooms began getting passed around, and Calysta collapsed into the grass, catching her breath as she ate them.

The water nymph who'd first given her wine sat next to her, summoning a small pool of moisture from the air and pushing it towards Calysta, who cupped it in her hands and drank.

"Thank you," she smiled.

The nymph's light blue skin flushed purple in her cheeks, and she brushed her silvery hair behind her shoulder. "Of course." She paused, pointed teeth dimpling her bottom lip as she surveyed the clearing with wide, black eyes. "Have you ever been to one of these before?"

Calysta nodded, watching as the other nymphs in the clearing began to settle. "A few times. Is this your first?"

"It is. I was born after the rites were outlawed."

The wonder in the younger nymph's face was shadowed by the anxiety of the unknown, and it plucked at the soft parts of Calysta's heart. She reached out to take her hand, light blue entwined with olive green. "Don't worry, you'll know what to do. Nethyl calls to us; just answer when you're ready." She smiled reassuringly before falling back into the grass, her free palm pressed to the ground.

The water nymph settled beside her, their hands still linked together, and Calysta watched the sky. Eventually, she let her magic wander, moving through the grass and moss around her as starlight sparkled in her eyes. Her mind slipped free along with her magic, sorting through memories and feelings and everything that was life.

Emotion swelled in her chest, love and sorrow and confusion and excitement all swirled through her as the light from the stars began to bleed and the moons started to spin in their place high above Nethyl. Curling her claws into the dirt, Calysta laughed at the fullness of her life—full of magic, full of adventure, full of people. People who she'd always felt the absence of, never knowing why a space in her felt so vacant until she'd met the ones who filled it.

Calysta took a deep, shuddering breath as spots of color twinkled among the stars, and she slipped back to a time four years prior when she'd found Aleah in the woods trying to grow a cherry tree.

A tiny sprout was just poking from the ground, and Aleah came every day to check on it, watering it and alternating between speaking soft, coaxing words and threatening it.

Intrigued, Calysta watched the redheaded half-fae. She'd never heard anyone try to barter for a plant's life with it before, and this girl amused her.

But then came a morning when Aleah didn't show up, and then a second. After waiting until the sun had climbed high in the sky, Calysta left her hiding place, sinking down next to the plant. "I'm sorry she forgot you, friend," she whispered, placing her palm to the ground and letting her magic spread around the tiny thing. Closing her eyes, she grew it into a sapling, making sure to send its roots deep and keep its trunk sturdy. "I should probably go now. I've lingered too long, but I hope to see you again one day."

Calysta had been so focused on the tree that she hadn't heard the approach of footsteps behind her. But she did hear the sharp intake of breath, leaping nearly out of her skin as she whirled around, raising her hands to call plants to her aide.

"Charles!" Aleah cried, hands flying to her mouth. Her hazel eyes were so wide with shock as she looked from Calysta to the sapling that they seemed to take up half of her freckled face. "Legends, look at you!" She ran over to the tree, lightly brushing her fingers over the dark, slender leaves before turning to Calysta with a bright smile. "You did this?"

Calysta took a step back, eyeing the wickedly curved knives strapped to the girl's waist. "Yes, I was going to leave the area and didn't want it to die if you'd also gone."

Aleah clasped her hands in front of her chest, looking back at the tree. "I was out of town on a job and didn't get back in until late last night. Thank you so much for watching her!"

"I'm sorry, but, um, did you call it Charles?"

"Yep! I decided it felt less weird talking to her if she had a name." Before Calysta could respond, Aleah reached out and grabbed her hand. "Hey, we've been trying to grow a garden on the rooftop back home. Would you mind coming to take a look and give me a few pointers? It's been pretty painful progress thus far."

The water nymph's fingers twitched in Calysta's hand, pulling her back to the present. She gave them a squeeze, sitting up and looking around the clearing. More time had gone by than she thought. "Can you feel the magic?"

The other nymph pressed both palms to the ground, nodding as droplets of dew began to rise from the grass and swirl around them. She looked at Calysta's hands with a bright smile. "It calls to me."

Calysta sighed contentedly, burying her own hands in the grass and sending her magic down into the ground. The nymphs in the clearing began humming a melody, soft at first, before turning into a chant. Calysta dug the claw of one thumb into her forearm, letting her blood spill free as she again braced her hands, looking up to the sky as her magic spiraled down to the ley line beneath them.

Even though she tried to prepare for it, the moment her magic was snagged by the river beneath her still took her breath away.

She gave to Nethyl, as Nethyl had given to her.

The nymphs remained focused on that innate connection; the magic flowing between them and the world, completely unaware that a few klicks north, where the festival was in full swing just outside of the city, a rift was torn between their realm and another.

Chapter 20

Nethyl calls to us

Eight years before …

LEONIDAS KNEW HE WAS special.

It wasn't cockiness that fueled his confidence, just the knowledge that he possessed a gift that was far better than any magic born to the fae. Even what he knew of the Keepers' power couldn't hold a flame to the instinct that ran through his own blood.

Leonidas knew birds, and birds knew him.

From the time he was a small boy, he was befriending and training the ravens that would raid his mother's garden. As a teen, he was working with the local couriers to train homing pigeons, stationing them strategically around Jekeida. Once he was first let into the castle aviary, it was over and done.

His fate was sealed.

He worked with them to train their falcons and hawks, but he had also built up a solid clientele around Umbra by that time, with many local farmers and hunters enlisting his help to train their birds. So when he was offered a job in the Royal Guard as a falconer, he politely declined, offering instead to sign a contract to continue to work with them, but also able to keep his individuality and autonomy to choose jobs outside of the Crown.

Though Leonidas had declined the Crown's invitation, he couldn't shake the image it had sparked in his head, filling his dreams with the idea of having his own aviary, training birds, keeping pigeons and ravens for messaging services, and doing rehab for avian wildlife around Jekeida. From that moment, he started saving as much as he could, spending only the bare minimum for room and board until he'd collected enough to purchase the aviary.

Horscha came a few months after. Leonidas had met her working with the messenger birds in Umbra. She didn't train the birds, but she'd always cared for them and had a way with keeping them calm and content.

Training birds was a learned skill—Leonidas could easily teach her how to teach them. But that special touch, the one the birds saw in a person, that was either there or not, which is why Leonidas propositioned her, prepared to offer much more than was probably wise, figuring he could earn her loyalty after the fact and it would all pay off in the end.

But much in the same way he had noticed Horscha's way with birds, she had also noticed him and knew of his reputation. Horscha accepted Leonidas' offer of employment with no negotiating.

From there, his already well-established reputation grew.

Leonidas was on his way back to Umbra after a job helping set up an aviary for messenger birds in East Audha, about to stop for the night when he heard the most horrendous shrieking, muffled by distance but unmistakable. He dropped from his horse, tying the reins around a tree branch and pulling a dagger from his belt.

He crept through the trees, listening to the keening animal. He knew from the cry that it was a chick, a raptor. It didn't take long for Leonidas to figure out why the cries sounded so angry and desperate. Blood and feathers littered the forest at his feet, and he leaned down to pick one up, spinning it in his fingers as his stomach dropped.

Leonidas tilted his head up. High in a pine was the nest, and he took a moment to look around again. A grown falcon had clearly been hunted here. He still worried about disturbing the nest in case the other parent returned, but by the screams coming from the chick left and the dried blood around him, it had been some time.

He decided it was safest to take a look, so he hauled himself into the tree, picking his way carefully up.

"Legends," Leonidas whispered, leaning back against a branch behind him, his body sagging.

Three chicks were in the nest. Two were dead, more than likely from hunger, the other resting heavily on the walls, head thrown back in a dramatic but effective manner as it used its last reserves of strength to call for help.

Leonidas reached in from beside and below, and the cries became even more wild, the hatchling lurching forward suddenly to fight him off.

"Don't panic, little friend." Leonidas spoke softly, scooping the bird to his chest and picking his way down the tree. Slowly, the bird's cries got quieter and quieter before they petered out.

He tucked the bird into his jacket after climbing back onto his horse, hurrying to the next town. He bought a flank of pork, setting up in the inn and mincing a portion of it. He scooped some of it up on the tip of his knife, holding it over where the bird had once again began its panicked cries, knowing that food was near.

Leonidas held the food over its mouth, pushing the meat off of the end of the knife.

When the bird was full, it quieted, blinking at him sleepily.

Leonidas laughed at the expression on its face, head dropped slightly to one side, big dark eyes staring from a fluffy white face, body poofed and crazy like a cloud. He curled a spare towel into a nest shape, placing the bird in its makeshift bed on the nightstand before going to sleep.

That first night, and a few nights after, when Leonidas was back in his aviary and letting the hatchling stay in his room, he was woken up multiple times by hungry shrieks, and quickly learned to keep extra minced meat on hand to easily and quickly quiet the bird.

After the first week, the falcon, which Leonidas had taken to calling Panic because of the wide, frozen way he looked at things upon first seeing them, started sprouting flight feathers, transitioning into a fledgling. Leonidas found himself itching for his first flight, and was already training him with small commands.

Panic knew the difference between which whistles meant come, stay, and go, and Leonidas was working on teaching him the silent hand signals for each.

One morning, Panic had hopped down from the platform Leonidas had crafted for him, molting wings flapping noisily as he tried to glide his way over. He walked along the stiff lines of Leonidas' legs until he was perched on the man's chest, peering down at him. He tapped the top of his beak against Leonidas' cheek with a soft chirrup.

Leonidas peeked an eye open. "Can I help you?"

Panic shrieked, spreading his wings. A tuft of downy white feathers flew from him with the movement.

Leonidas stood, letting Panic tumble down his chest. The bird glared at him, but sat quietly as he got dressed. After sliding into his jacket, Leonidas held out an arm, letting Panic climb up to his shoulder, wings flapping around unhelpfully. "You're going to have to figure that out soon," he told the bird.

He left Panic on a counter with a field mouse, which the fledgling was happily and messily tearing into, as he went about his morning routine with the other birds in the aviary, spreading breakfast and replacing cage linings. When that was finished, he went downstairs, where Horscha was just showing up with a basket that smelled of bread and meat.

"Breakfast?" she greeted, setting the basket down on the counter.

Panic, who'd hopped down after Leonidas, *kak'd* from the floor, looking from one to the other.

"What would I do without you?" Leonidas said in thanks, scooping up the falcon and setting him on the counter before taking a seat.

"Starve, but your birds would thrive," Horscha answered, rolling her eyes. "Morning, screamies." She scratched Panic's chest.

"He's gotten much quieter the past week," Leonidas remarked around a mouthful of food, elbows propped on the counter as he leaned forward to eat.

Horscha raised a dark brow, grabbing a link of sausage for herself. "He makes a noise almost every time you talk to him."

Leonidas looked at Panic, who blinked, shaking out his feathers. A few more tufts of down floated through the air. "That's called a conversation," he told Horscha.

Panic cried his agreement.

"You're spoiling him, you know that, right?"

"He's a baby; you can't spoil a baby."

Horscha gave him an appraising look. "I don't think the falcon imprinted on you. I think you imprinted on the falcon."

Leonidas held out a hand toward Panic, who spread his toes and slapped his foot against Leonidas' fingers a couple times. "We're just buds, that's all."

"What's the plan for today?"

"I'll be heading just out of town to one of the farms. Someone picked up a hawk from a trader that passed through recently. Was told it was trained for hunting, but either it hasn't been trained or the farmer doesn't know how to command it. I'm not sure which is more likely, to be honest."

"Don't forget to grab food if you're out late," Horscha ordered, replacing him behind the counter as he readied himself for departure, strapping a few knives to his belt and letting Panic climb back up to his shoulder.

"Promise." Leonidas waved her off as he walked out the door.

"You did so good today, buddy," Leonidas spoke quietly to the bird on his shoulder as he walked down the street.

Panic knew the tone of praise, and puffed his little chest out.

"That hawk was probably twice your age, and look how much better you already know commands. The smartest bird on all of Nethyl. I'd put money on it." Leonidas' stomach rumbled, and he realized he had once again gotten carried away, lost in his work, and was now starving.

Stopping, he weighed his options. A part of his male pride didn't want to go to the aviary to drop off Panic, because then Horscha would know he'd once again skipped a meal until his body screamed at him for food. But he couldn't take the falcon into an eatery. "You ready for a real test?"

Panic chirruped.

Leonidas found an establishment with high planters outside, setting the bird down on an edge, and giving him both the signal and sound for stay.

Panic blinked at him, shifting on his feet as he settled in.

Leonidas ordered food at the counter and snagged a table by a window where he could keep an eye on Panic. It wasn't the bird wandering off that he worried about, but people walking by who might mess with him.

Before long, an almost ridiculous amount of food was placed in front of Leonidas, but he was a large and active man, and he hungrily tucked in.

Halfway through his meal, he was approached by a male with dark skin and darker wings, tightly twisted locs of hair spilling over his shoulders. "You own the new aviary, right?"

Leonidas nodded.

"Do you mind if I sit?"

Leonidas gestured to the seat across from him, taking another bite.

"My name is Jasper. I've been working as a mercenary for the past five years and was wondering if you'd be interested in setting up a contract of sorts."

"You own the building next to mine," Leonidas said, stripping a chunk of chicken from bone.

"Yes, I do."

"That red-headed kid. She's with you, too?"

"She is."

Leonidas took a long drink before meeting Jasper's silver gaze. "What kind of a contract?"

"You could call it a right to first choice." Jasper folded his hands in front of him on the table. "I would ask that if you hear word of any potential work in Nethyl, anything that might be in our ... wheelhouse, you bring it to us first before potentially selling the information to anyone else. In exchange, we would provide a set finder's fee for any jobs we accept and use only your aviary for any of our needs in that area."

Leonidas narrowed his eyes, Jasper still holding his gaze. "Anything that might be in your wheelhouse?" he questioned. His eyes flicked to the window, Panic sitting where Leonidas had left him, quietly watching the light traffic on the street.

Jasper spread his hands in an expression of openness. "It's always been the people in power who have pushed their moral boundaries on others, while often not following it themselves. I won't tell you that everything I do is above board, but there is too much that goes on in the world for everyone to follow some nuanced, socially enforced code of conduct."

"I'm not judging, by any means," Leonidas assured him. "Just making sure I understand what you're asking."

"I just want to fix some of the injustices in the world without all the political setbacks," Jasper leaned back, wings spreading to give him room.

Leonidas ate quietly for a few more moments. "I think we can work something out."

"And I can trust in your discretion?"

"My birds might hear things, but I promise they're good secret keepers." Leonidas joked.

Jasper laughed, reaching out to shake his hand. "I'll draw something up tonight. Come over at any time tomorrow to sign it."

Chapter 22

Wear some iron

SHILOH WALKED DOWN THE streets of Umbra, hands tucked into their pockets and a joint hanging, unlit, from their pierced lips. Even without the fragrant smoke filling their lungs, calming their mind, they still felt more calm with it held in their mouth.

It had been four days since the full moons festival had ended in terror, creatures breaking through from another world and taking the little prince with them. And Bellamy ... Shiloh sighed, running a hand through their dark hair. They hoped he was handling everything better than when they'd last seen him. His eyes had been so flat, completely lacking the lively glimmer they'd seen when talking to him at the festival. But he was gone now, off searching for a way to bring Ryddan back, and Shiloh hoped the active response was helping to keep the Ranger from another spiral.

Surprisingly, the citizens of Umbra had settled down fairly quickly after the attack. There had been utter chaos and fear that night, but after only a day, people had started to resume their normal routines.

"The demonslayer is taking care of it," Shiloh overheard one fae telling another. "And the king's gone to consult Her Majesty Regenya. He'll do right by us."

The other nodded definitively. "I'll tell you what, though. I'm glad to have her watching over things here. I was saying even a few years back that she was outgrowing her nickname."

"The prince's pet, now the reason we roam the streets without worry. Who'd have thought it?"

Because the people of Umbra were so keen to go back to normal life, Shiloh also decided they may as well continue their scheduled performances and make a bit more money before heading back home.

A cold gust of air blew through the square, plastering the cloak to their back and pinning their delicate wings uncomfortably. They turned, peering into the wind. Tears sprung to their eyes against the icy blast, their dark hair whipped around their face. Something felt off. They couldn't identify why, but they suddenly felt ... uncomfortable.

Dark clouds loomed over the mountains, rolling swiftly toward Umbra with the wind.

"Fuck me," Shiloh muttered, holding their cloak tighter about them. Umbra was nowhere near as large as Do Lech, but the streets that veered off from the main center felt like a maze to them. They knew their home like the veins in their wings, but the royal city had them all turned about.

They saw a sign above the door ahead of them and ducked through without bothering to read it.

The loss of the wind at their back was an instant relief, and they fluttered their wings, no longer flattened between fabrics. Though the wind was gone and the air in the building was warm, it was far from quiet. Soft chirps and occasional screeches filled the building, along with an almost constant flapping. Shiloh's gaze landed on the staircase across from them, blocked off by a thick rope hung with a sign that simply said *no*.

"Can I help you?" a soft voice asked, and they moved their eyes to the female sitting behind a counter, three pigeons on a perch cooing behind her.

"Yes, please." Shiloh stepped forward, pulling the joint from their lips and tucking it into a pocket on their vest. "I'm looking for a performance theater, The Majestic?"

"Ah, yes, that one is a few streets down. Hold on, let me draw you up some directions."

Footsteps sounded on the stairs, and Shiloh turned to see a tall, blonde man step over the rope.

"You said you're going to The Majestic?" he asked.

Shiloh nodded.

"I'm headed that way. I can point you in the right direction if you'd like."

"That would be much appreciated, thank you."

"Not a problem." Leonidas gave them a brief smile before turning to the Horscha. "I'll be out for the night. Mind closing up?"

"Not at all."

"Clean up after them," he said, pointing a finger at the pigeons. "I don't know how you favor them when they're such a damn mess."

She laughed, looking behind her at the three birds. One tilted its head to and fro. "Cute little empty-headed babies. They like me."

Leonidas let out a sharp, short whistle as he walked to the door, Shiloh flinching at the noise as a falcon flew down the staircase, lighting on his shoulder. "Sorry, I forget to warn people."

Shiloh gave a short laugh as they stepped back outside. The heavy gusts had died down, but wind still pulled through the street, and they were eternally grateful when Leonidas led them down an alley, the buildings blocking the wind.

"You're that performer from Do Lech, right? With the magic tricks?"

Shiloh blinked, but their surprise was quickly washed away when they realized that, of course, they would be recognizable. Not many people in Umbra dressed like them. "I am."

"Bellamy is obsessed with you." Leonidas chuckled. Then he stopped, looking down at Shiloh in slight alarm as he realized what he said. "Not in a creepy way. He's just very impressed with what you do. Awestruck. In a normal way. He brought us to watch one of your routines at the full moons festival."

Shiloh laughed, warmth filling them at the knowledge the Ranger had been talking about them. "A fucking nugget, that one."

Leonidas was confused at the title, but shrugged, deciding that it probably fit. "My partner was very impressed as well, couldn't stop theorizing about how you pulled some of that off. He's ... well, he also makes a living by having quick fingers. I'm Leo, by the way."

"Shiloh."

"That's right. Sorry, I'm not the best with names. Mer must've said it a dozen times after she got back from Do Lech."

Shiloh followed him down a bend in the street. "Do you know everyone in Umbra?"

"What? No. Well, possibly. But Mer was one of us before she became marshal. Then Ryddan—" he paused, running a hand over his hair as a wave of worry flooded his chest. *They're looking. They'll find him.* "He stayed with us for a while last year, and Bell brings him by to visit every now and then. Panic likes him." Leonidas added the last bit as if that were as much information as anyone should ever need about a situation.

"Panic?"

The falcon shrieked in response, hopping to Leonidas' other shoulder to see if he was being offered a snack.

"Oh," Shiloh laughed, looking up at the powerful bird.

"You're performing tonight?" Leonidas asked, turning down another street.

"All week," they replied, looking behind them with a slight unease at the prospect of whether or not they'd be able to make it back to their inn at the end of the night.

"Don't worry, the main street isn't too hard to find from the theater. You'll only have a problem if you're trying to make it back to the aviary," Leonidas assured them. He turned down another street and pointed to his left. "The Majestic is right up there. To get back to the main road, you'll want to—"

Panic's feathers fluffed out, his head turning to peer behind him. After two clicks of his beak, he lifted into the air, smacking Leonidas in the face with a wing.

He soared up into the sky, not fighting the wind as it pushed him back, but climbing through it, waiting until he was above the current to fly back over where Leonidas stood with the stranger who knew his name. He peered at the ground, hearing Leonidas whistle for him and seeing the hand motions that commanded him down.

Panic spun up with a long shriek, leveling back out and continuing to watch. Something was wrong. That pull was back, like that long-buried instinct to follow the warmth in the winter, but different.

There, from the south, were two shapes, using the wind at their backs to push them quickly through the air, their wings large and carrying them quickly across the distance.

It was those horrible, hideous byrds. Ones like what had taken Ryddan. Panic spiraled high into the sky as the first grew close. Air ripped past his feathers with a sound like tearing paper as he dove. He flared his wings and threw his feet forward, talons spread wide, as he slammed into the creature.

"PANIC, NO!" Leonidas yelled from the ground. He'd completely forgotten Shiloh beside him, his eyes on his falcon as Panic attacked.

The creature rocked to the side with a violent screech, and drops of black blood splashed on the ground from where Panic's talons had torn into its neck. Leonidas watched helplessly as Panic held fast to the creature that was more than twice his size, wings flapping as he ducked his head in, beak tearing at the byrd's face and neck.

A second byrd appeared, dipping low into the streets, followed by a cloud of oily black smoke that chilled Leonidas' blood. He pulled a sword from a sheath at his back. "Get out of here," he said to Shiloh, a deadly calm in his voice.

Shiloh took a few steps back into the alley without questioning.

The byrd Panic attacked fell to the ground, and Leonidas watched the falcon whirl toward the second. He gave another sharp whistle, ordering the Panic away from his prey.

Panic looked at him, knowing the sword in Leonidas' hand meant that he understood danger was near, and banked heavily, curving away from the other byrd and perching on the building next to Leonidas, his bright, golden eyes still watching the creature's movement.

Leonidas lost sight of the unformed demon, but he saw the byrd dive toward a family that was walking along the street.

"Down!" he hollered at them from a dead sprint.

But they were not fighters, and only looked back at him, first in confusion and then terror at the weapon in his hands.

The byrd clipped the top of the father's head, blood welling from his scalp where a claw had scraped him. Its foot locked around the mother's hair, dragging her sideways with a scream.

Fucking civilians, Leonidas thought, throwing one hand out to push the female down and out of the way as he ripped his sword upward in a deadly arc. It split the belly of the demon open, black blood raining down on his arm and covering the fae.

She and the child were screaming, the noise almost more piercing than the anguished cry of the byrd as it crashed into the road, flapping its wings feebly as a string of intestines spilled from its gut.

Leonidas walked up to it, spinning his sword in his hand before he brought it down over its neck, severing its head. He grimaced as he wiped the blood from the steel, knowing he'd have to spend a good amount of time honing the edge that had bitten into the pavement, but he pushed the irritation to the back of his mind, scanning the street.

The few people who were about looked at him with wide eyes, terror plain on their faces. His gaze skipped over them, barely registering as he looked for signs of where the unformed demon had gone, then up to the sky, waiting to see if anything else was coming.

When the wind brought no more assailants, he looked down at his arm and slung it, disgust curling his lips as droplets of acrid black blood splattered against the street. He lifted his clean hand, signaling to Panic that he was free to come down, and the falcon glided towards him, landing with a hop next to the fallen byrd, head cocking as he inspected it.

His beak and talons were covered in the dark blood from his attack on the other, but despite having the foul liquid on him, he curiously braced a foot against the byrd's chest, leaning forward to rip free a chunk of flesh.

"Legends," Leonidas muttered as the bird threw his head back to swallow the meat, then frantically shook his head, clicking his beak and hopping back from the body. "For being so smart, sometimes you're really, really dumb," he told Panic, who looked at him with an accusing glare. "I didn't tell you to eat it." Leonidas shrugged, turning to where Shiloh peeked from the alley, their fingers curled around the corner of the building.

"These are the same things that attacked the festival. What the Hel are they?" they asked, stepping warily into the street.

"Bad news," Leonidas answered, walking up to them. "Listen, can you fly?"

Shiloh, the wind blowing their hair across their face, nodded, brows knit in confusion.

"I'm going to send Panic back to the merc house. Follow him. Jasper, big guy, black wings, should be there. Tell him the demons came back. He should know where to find—" he broke off, his chest tightening at the thought of Campbell wandering town with that demon on the loose. He swallowed against the urge to find him first. "He should know where to find everyone else. I'm going to the castle to report to the captain and get a bird sent to the king."

Shiloh nodded. "Jasper, wings, demons are back."

"And wear some iron if you have any. The more the better."

Shiloh lifted their hand to a heavily pierced ear. "Ahead of the game for once."

Leonidas cracked a small smile, then whistled for Panic, giving him the signal to head home, and Shiloh pulled their cloak free and lifted off to follow him. Their slender wings, so delicate in appearance, were surprisingly powerful, cutting through the wind to follow the falcon without issue.

Leonidas slid his sword back into his scabbard, heading up the hill toward the castle at a full sprint.

The guards at the gates stood as he approached, alarmed at his speed. "Where's Captain Dio?" he panted.

"I think he's training in the courtyard," one answered.

Leonidas nodded, barreling past and around to the back of the castle. As he skidded to a stop, he realized one sleeve of his shirt was completely stained with blood, and small pricks of tightness on his skin told him blood had spattered and dried on his face as well.

A few of the Guard turned their attention to him as he stopped at the edge of the training ring, chest heaving. At the pause of their comrades, more turned to look at him, training coming to a full halt.

Dio turned around, lowering his sword and walking over as soon as he saw Leonidas.

"They came back," Leonidas said once the newly appointed captain was close enough to hear without his words being ripped away in the wind. "From the south."

Dio's hand tightened around the hilt of his practice sword, alarm sparking in his eyes.

"Two of those flying creatures, both dispatched, but a demon as well. Unformed. I lost sight of it."

Dio stiffened, motioning for two guardsmen to come closer. "Go tell the commanders I need to meet with them. We'll be patrolling Umbra tonight. Have them wait in my office."

They nodded, saluting before running off.

Dio grabbed Leonidas' elbow, pulling him further away from the ring. "These were the same kind that took the prince?"

Leonidas nodded, about to run a hand over his hair before re-membering it was coated in dried blood. "And the demon the same that attacked last summer. I was going to send a bird to Entumbra, but wanted to make sure you knew about the demon still loose."

Dio's jaw ticked, his teeth clenching together almost hard enough to crack. "We need the king back here, and soon."

"Even the fastest raven will take a day to reach them," Leonidas said.

"Tell them to Travel back. This might have just been a test, a trial run to see how easily they can open a portal now that they have Ryddan, but if they've broken through again, they won't wait long."

"Will do. I sent a messenger to the mercenaries. They'll be out searching, as well."

Dio nodded. "Thank you. I'm grateful for your expertise and assistance."

"This is our home, too." Leonidas rested a hand on the captain's shoulder. "We've a personal interest in keeping it safe."

Chapter 23

Because of Kodi

EVEN COMBINING THEIR EFFORTS, neither the mercenaries nor the Guard had been able to find the demon, but Merriam and Mollian had returned to Umbra, and they'd located the realm of the demons that kept invading their home.

Kodi came home the night they returned, collapsing onto the couch with his head in Aleah's lap. "They're organizing the Guard to march south."

"When?" Leonidas asked, looking up from where he sat with his sword and a whetting stone.

"Tomorrow. I guess there's a spot to the south where some really weird things are happening to the trees, and they think it's worth the bet that that's where the demons will try to break through." Kodi's eyes fluttered closed as Aleah ran her fingers through his hair. "Mer's making everyone iron necklaces to protect against possession."

"I'm surprised you assholes are okay with the prospect of fighting without your magic," Aleah joked to force through the fear that churned in her stomach.

"Don't worry, I can always take it off if I feel the need."

Aleah tugged on his hair, scowling at him. "Don't you even fucking dare."

Kodi winced, peeking one eye open and smiling. "Okay, okay, I'll wear my silly little necklace."

"I'll go up to the castle tomorrow and talk to the captain," Jasper said. "We're coming to help, of course."

Leonidas nodded, lifting his sword to eye level to examine the edge.

"We should be nominated for Legendom with how much we've saved Sekha," Aleah said with a wry grin. The prospect of a large-scale battle scared her, but in a way she was used to. The mercenary knew herself well enough not to worry about being able to funnel that anxious energy into the deadly dance of a fight.

She was walking through Umbra the next morning, gathering a few supplies for Leonidas while he helped out at the castle aviary, when she overheard a conversation that stopped her in her tracks. "What did you say?" she asked, not even realizing she had her hand wrapped around a fae's wrist in a death grip.

The male had at first looked angry, but it had morphed to unease at the force of her grip and the manic light in her eyes. "Overseer Kinbriar and his wife arrived in town yesterday," he repeated cautiously.

Aleah released him, blinking rapidly in an attempt to focus herself. "Do you know why they're here?"

The male shrugged, rubbing his wrist and shooting a look to his companion. "No, just that they've petitioned to speak with the king."

Aleah stumbled back a few steps before spinning away and hurrying down the street. Her grandparents. In Umbra.

Because of Kodi, she thought, her heart seizing. *We have to protect him.* She ran back to the merc house, errands forgotten.

Aleah barreled through the back door, bounding up the stairs into the office.

Jasper looked up, watching as she pressed her back against the wall and slid to the floor, wrapping her arms around her knees and resting her chin on them. He waited, letting her mull over her thoughts, sorting through them and figuring out what emotion she was actually experiencing and why.

Finally, her eyes flicked to his, and she sighed, tipping her head back against the wall. "You know what's kind of funny when you think about it? How much I hid when I first left home. I tried to never stay in one place for long or let anyone see my hair. I didn't want to be recognizable in case my family tried to come after me." She rolled her lip between her teeth, dropping her gaze to the floor. "They never did, though. I completely disappeared from their lives, and I don't think anyone ever set foot outside of Do Lech in search of me."

There was a weighted pause before she continued, tears and disdain filling her eyes. "My grandparents knew every horrible thing Chetney did to me, and I don't even want to imagine the things he may have done to others, but I'm sure they knew about all of that, too. He was wicked and slimy and vile, but they came for him. Not even just scouts or representatives, but dragged their own self-important asses all the way here to petition the Crown." She sniffed, wiping the heel of her hand across her cheek to catch the tears that had fallen and angrily blinking away the rest.

"Even after everything that happened, some part of me thought that maybe they'd cared. But they never saw me as anything more than he did," she said softly. "I think that's what gets me the most. He was a massive pile of shit, and he was mean and merciless and terrifying. I think ... I think because of how brutal he was, I never realized that they're the giant assholes that produced that pile of shit."

Jasper moved from the desk to sit on the floor in front of her, resting a hand on her knees. "Have I ever told you how proud of you I am?" Aleah scoffed, rolling her eyes, but Jasper continued. "All of you are amazing, and I wake up every day feeling lucky to have landed this little family of ours. For almost a decade, I've watched you dominate every single obstacle and challenge in your path. Fuzzy morals aside, you're probably one of the most respected assassins in the country. And even with everything you've been through, you're still one of the brightest sparks on this fucking planet. You love strong and hard. You're loyal. You're funny and feral and haven't let yourself be jaded out of fierce friendships and a love that would honestly have me worried if you were anyone else." She snorted a laugh, and he cracked a smile.

"I say all of this so you know that I'm not just talking out of my ass when I tell you that neglecting to protect you and missing out on having you be part of their lives is the worst mistake they've ever made. From the bottom of my heart, fuck them. They don't deserve you."

Fresh tears lined Aleah's eyes, and she leaned forward to throw her arms around Jasper's neck. "You and the others are the only family I ever needed. You're the only family I claim." She let him hold her for a moment before pulling away to fiercely wipe the tears from her cheeks. "Wanna do some fact-checking with me? I think I know how to send them running back home, no violence required."

"Whatever you need, red."

It had taken slightly longer than anticipated for Aleah to find what she'd needed. The fact that most census and law books were dryer than a week-old biscuit didn't help anything, but she eventually found what she was looking for.

She and Jasper stayed behind when the others left, promising to catch up soon. She hadn't told any of them that her grandparents had come, especially not Kodi. They were headed towards real danger, and she didn't want them distracted or worried about her because of Spiro and Larna. They were *her* problem, and she would take care of it.

"Are you sure you want to go alone?" Jasper asked as she raked her fire-red hair into a ponytail.

"They can't hurt me. They were never the ones that held power over me to begin with. I'll be fine," she assured him, tying off her hair and stepping out the door.

Aleah hadn't been lying when she said she felt okay. It was almost like with the threat of Chetney gone, her fears felt so much smaller. Her grandparents had never protected her, but her uncle was the only monster that had ever haunted her in the dark.

But as she walked up the steps of the inn toward her grandparents' suite, a small knot of nervousness wound tight in her belly. Maybe she should have allowed Jasper to come with her.

"Chetney is dead," she whispered to the small voice trying to fill her with fear. "He can't hurt us anymore." Then she squared her shoulders, palming the hilt of her favorite citrus-carved knife, and knocked.

Spiro opened the door, and the ghost of a smile twitched across Aleah's lips. She remembered her grandfather as such a large, strong presence, someone it took balls to stand up against. But the male in front of her looked old, his posture tired and defeated.

Because of Kodi, she thought, warm satisfaction rippling through her.

Spiro was staring at her, slack-jawed in his surprise. Aleah smiled sweetly, batting her lashes. "Hello, Grandfather," she said, pushing past him.

Larna was sitting on a settee on the other side of the room, and her face went completely white when she saw Aleah. Her hands even shook a bit. Aleah sauntered over and plopped down next to her, barely holding back something like a purr, but unable to keep the elation from flashing in her eyes. "You remember me, then?"

Larna's eyes flicked to Spiro only for a moment before returning to Aleah, afraid to lose sight of her for long.

"This is a surprise, Aleah," Spiro said, clearing his throat.

Aleah pulled a knife from her belt, pressing the tip to her finger and spinning it as she turned her attention to him. "I can imagine, considering you've been telling people I fucking drowned. Death looks good on me, wouldn't you say?"

"You disappeared," Larna said quietly. "We had to tell people something."

Aleah snorted loudly. "I disappeared? Did you know that I left, or did you figure Chetney had finally taken it too far and actually killed me?"

"He was getting better," Spiro sputtered without much conviction.

A wave of anger washed over Aleah, and she narrowed her gaze on Spiro in a cold, predatory glare. A spark of true fear lit in his hazel eyes, and he swallowed roughly. Satisfaction ran an electric current through her veins, but her voice was low and measured when she spoke. "I came here to have a civil conversation, but defend that Legend-forsaken asswipe one more time and I will give you a set of scars to match those he gave me."

She looked from Spiro to Larna, and when neither of them spoke again, she nodded, slipping her knife back into her belt and hopping to her feet with a clap of her hands. The quick flip in her attitude only served to scare the two fae more. "Now, a little birdie told me that the two of you were hoping to bring some sort of complaint to the Crown, but I don't think that's really necessary."

"This has nothing to do with you, Aleah. An envoy from Umbra came to Do Lech, and two people were dead when they left. We simply want justice," Spiro said.

"We didn't even know you were in Umbra," Larna added hastily, hands folded in her lap to keep from trembling.

Aleah rolled her eyes dramatically. "It's got *everything* to do with me. I've heard about my dear uncle's disappearance, of course. If you'd truly thought I was dead, it's understandable why you never tried to find me or have someone come bring me home to get settled. I can forgive you that small oversight. In that regard, it's incredibly lucky that I happened to be here when the two of you showed up."

Spiro steeled his shoulders, refusing to give her any outward sign that she terrified him.

A good hunter could always sniff out fear, though, and Aleah had had years to cultivate that sense. She smiled her brightest, most sinister smile. "Forgive me if I'm misremembering—you'll understand that most of my memories from childhood are muddied by pain and fear—but my mother was older than Chetney, wasn't she?" Aleah tilted her head to the side, tapping a finger against her chin. "Yes, I believe that's right. And the laws that govern Do Lech are extremely specific when it comes to succession, which I *do* know for a fact. Just like I know they dictate that the position of Overseer is passed down from firstborn to firstborn, regardless of gender. It only passes on to a sibling if the firstborn never conceived a child."

"Aleah," Spiro said carefully, holding his hands up placatingly.

She ignored him, spinning on her heel and walking over to the window. "Regardless of where my uncle went and if he ever comes back, I am the rightful heir to Do Lech." She turned back around, leaning casually against the wall with her arms crossed over her chest. "Now, the way I see it, there are two options for how we proceed here. Option one, you plead your case to whomever it is King Mollian left in charge, and I meet you back in Do Lech, where I will claim my rightful place as heir and tell everyone where I've been all these years and *precisely* why I left. I've grown into quite the storyteller, if I do say so myself, and I promise you that I will spare no detail of what I recall from childhood nor fail to name all who knew of it." Aleah paused, letting the weight of the threat sink in for a moment.

Spiro stepped closer to Larna, who reached out to clasp his hand. He wet his lips with a small shake of his head, swallowing.

"Or there's option two," she continued before he could speak. "You accept that Chetney is gone and Illiziana's death was an unfortunate casualty of faulty politics and go home. Aleah Kinbriar remains in her watery grave, and succession moves to one of your other children—hopefully one who's capable of empathy and less prone to violence than their older brother. Or niece." She flashed a brilliant smile as she finished. "Is it nature or nurture, do you think, that allows us to draw blood from others without any true remorse? Don't answer that, actually. I've had my fill of ... reminiscing for the night, and I have more important places to be. Make your choice, and I'll be on my way."

Spiro shook his head slowly, dragging his hands over his face. "Did you ..." He swallowed, unable to voice his question.

"Did I kill him?" Aleah asked for him, pushing away from the wall. "No. Now choose."

Her grandparents looked at each other for a moment before Spiro turned back to her. "We will return home. We won't petition the Crown," he said quietly.

Aleah was surprised to find that some small part of her had hoped that they might have wanted her back, even if it meant admitting everything they'd allowed Chetney to do. But the bitterness that pricked at her faded almost as soon as she'd recognized it. They truly weren't worth the energy of a grudge. "Very well. I suggest you stick to the main roads, away from the ley lines."

She'd made it all the way to the door before her grandmother spoke up. "Aleah, wait." She did, hand on the doorknob, but turned slightly to face the tired-eyed female. "Who did you become when you left us? Are you ... are you happy?"

Aleah blinked, some of the harshness leaving her face. She looked so much like her mother in that moment that Larna's eyes filled with tears. "I became someone who could easily take the hands from anyone that tried to lay them on me, someone with a family who would kill to protect me ... someone who is no longer afraid of love." She gave them both one last look, a sad smile stretching her lips. "I suspect that you will often think of me now that you know I escaped, that a piece of your daughter is still out in the world, thriving. But understand that once I know you're gone from this city, I will never think of you again, and my world will be brighter for it."

Then she left, slipping out onto the streets of Umbra with a lightness in her chest that made her giddy. It was all she could manage not to skip back to the merc house. Though she would wait to make sure her grandparents left, she was eager to follow her friends south to battle.

Chapter 24

If Nethyl falls

FOUR DAYS INTO THE march south, Sekha's Royal Guard reached the expanse of ground that would soon become a battlefield.

They crested a hill to find every tree in the vicinity drained of life. Not dead, just decimated. Calysta left Merriam and Mollian on the hilltop, heading down into the forest with her heart in her stomach. These trees were wrong.

She stumbled as she walked into them, their massacred leaves triggering a volatile reaction full of more violence than she could ever recall feeling before. She pushed her fingers into the ground, her magic falling from the tips and into the earth below her, down into the roots of the aspens.

Worms, she thought, glancing up. The leaves were marked with paths where they'd been eaten, drained of color, and when her magic brushed against the trees, she knew that whatever had caused it was not from their realm. The demons were killing her planet, and she wouldn't allow it to continue.

Calysta walked through the grove, hands flung out to either side of her. She pushed the demon bugs from the trees with her magic, doing her best to heal them as she wandered. Had the other nymphs somehow not seen this? Had they not been able to feel the otherworldly hunger that was eating away at the leaves?

The wood nymph eventually reached a river, where she plucked a long blade of grass and tied it into a knot. She pricked the tip on one finger with the claw of another, dotting her sparkling blood to the knot and dropping it into the water.

Then she sat and waited. Before long, a water nymph broke the surface, her blue skin sparkling in the sunlight and water streaming from her pale green hair.

"I need to speak with the elders," Calysta told her. "Without delay."

"Whom should I tell them is requesting they gather?" the other nymph asked.

"Calysta, nymph of the southern woods and the central mountains."

The water nymph nodded before sliding off to pass the message, and Calysta sat at the river bank to wait.

When the nymph returned, she led Calysta further into the woods, past the areas affected by the worms and further still with no conversation between them. Finally, they reached a small clearing where three old nymphs sat: one wood, one water, and one wild. Other nymphs had also gathered around the edges of the clearing, curious about the request.

"Who are you to call us here?" the old wood nymph asked, eyes traveling over Calysta like she was entirely unimpressed. "You who have left us to commune with the fae. You smell of them and their false sense of superiority."

Calysta twisted her hands into the folds of her short dress, bowing her head in deference. "I come humbly before you to plead for help. Nethyl is under attack by a demon realm, which can plainly be seen by the trees and the parasitic creatures harming them. The Keeper Mollian, King of Sekha, has traveled south to fight against the demon invasion, and I have come to request aid."

"You ask to make warriors of the folk?" the water nymph hissed, outraged.

"We do not participate in wars, young one. This sounds like a problem for the fae to figure out. The folk do not get involved in such trivial matters."

"It's not trivial!" Calysta insisted, resisting the urge to stamp her foot in frustration. "It's not just the fae's problem. Have you not seen the trees?

These demons want to take Nethyl's magic for their own. We have to do what we can to help make sure that doesn't happen."

"She's right," Novi spoke up, pushing their way through the crowd, and Calysta almost sagged with relief at seeing her old friend. "You've said yourselves that you don't understand why the trees are turning against us. Calysta knows the Keepers. She knows the halfling that rid us of Illiziana's nuisance. You think she's a traitor to our ways because she lives as one of the fae, but she's in a better position to understand what's happening around Sekha and the way it affects us all than any of you. The connections she's made are important. When was the last time any of you saw a king march south with an army? Do you not remember reports of the creatures from last summer? The ones that killed Prince Oren? We helped Orym learn the ways of the Gate so that he could protect Nethyl for us. We must honor that by helping his descendant now. If Nethyl falls, we fall with her."

The wood nymph elder shook her head, lips pressed together. "You speak with baseless authority, Novi. You may be a successor, but I am not dead yet. The council will decide if Calysta's claims hold true and if this situation calls for the nymphs' interference."

The water nymph nodded, straightening his shoulders. "We will discuss the nymphs' place in this war," he said. "Nethyl is our stewardship, and if she is truly in the danger you say, then we will do what we can to keep her from harm."

"She is." Calysta cursed the desperation in her voice, clenching her hands together to hide the way they trembled.

"We will discuss, as promised, and decide in due time." The wild nymph answered with such finality that Calysta bit off her response for fear of annoying them into declining.

There was no time, but that was no longer something in her control.

Novi approached her as the elder nymphs drifted off. "Do you want to stay with me tonight?" they asked, gently taking Calysta's hand.

She looked down at their twined fingers, Novi's a slightly deeper green. Her first and oldest friend. She squeezed their hand, finally meeting their eyes. "I need to go back to the camp and prepare for my part in this fight."

Novi studied her thoughtfully for a moment. "You really do love them, don't you?"

"Yes," Calysta answered simply. "They're my family."

Epilogue
You watch the skies

CALYSTA RETURNED TO CAMP, unsure whether or not her people would help, but happy to be back with the mercenaries. Though she was still nervous, she trusted that Novi was out there arguing in favor of joining the fight, and already she felt more settled, preparing alongside people she'd fought with many times before.

After their customary game of Odds, they sat around a fire reorganizing and double-checking their weapons while Merriam braided each of their hair in turn. The fight could come at any moment, and they would be prepared.

"Are you sure you don't want more knives? Or maybe something with more range?" Jasper asked, refitting the final knife into Calysta's belt before handing it over.

She laughed. "Jasper, are you trying to weigh me down? You know I'm not going to use all of these. I have my magic. Nethyl is my weapon."

"A blade is more evenly matched to a demon's claws than a sprig of bramble," he said softly.

She met his eyes with a confident smirk. "Let me worry about that. You watch the skies, bird boy."

Before Jasper could retort, Rovin and Kodi called for a ring to be formed, everyone more than ready to burn off some nervous energy instead of sitting around all night.

Calysta smiled, watching Merriam drop from Rovin's back, firelight dancing in her eyes as she pulled her axes free and twirled them around, already taunting and dancing on her feet.

Standing at the edge of the ring, she watched the friendly competition, first between Merriam and Mollian, then Kodi and Jasper, the jokes and banter almost non-stop amidst attacks as others called out challenges to each other for the next round.

She took a deep breath, letting herself feel the full breadth of how much she loved these people. Fear of what might come had no power against the strength of the bond she shared with the mercenaries or the warmth of contentment that spread through her with the acknowledgment of it. Without a doubt, the battle against the demons would be the most dangerous fight any of them had ever been in, but as the raucous laughter and back-and-forth comments filled the night air, Calysta knew that there was nowhere else she would rather be.

Acknowledgements

This is it: the end of an era. Fully and truly this time, and I don't even know how to comprehend or break down what I'm feeling. I've spent countless late nights, early mornings, and long drives with Merriam, Mollian, and the rest of these characters in my head, urging me to tell this part of their story. In retrospect, it's only been about two years, but they were damn-near constant companions, and I'm not quite sure how to go about leaving them behind to fully move on to the next group. It's the most bittersweet goodbye, and I wouldn't have been able to do it without giving the mercenaries their own proper send-off. When I started writing *Leaves*, I never expected the mercs to mean so much to me, but each one of them has a little piece of my soul. I hope you found something relatable in them, too.

First and foremost, thank you to every single one of you who picked up *Leaves*, *Mountains*, and *Conduct*. With all of the books in the world, thank you for taking a chance on mine, for spending your time in my world. It means so much more than I could ever express, and I wouldn't be here without you and your support!

There's a few people who this novella never would have happened without. Sarah M (Sarah B? "Saraaaabiii" - Scar), you were the first person to suggest that maybe this story didn't belong in *Mountains*. It was hard to hear, but you were absolutely right, and I needed you to tell me because I never would have forced it on my own. Your support, honesty, and love for me and my characters warms my whole Cancer heart. Mursiel, I can't even count the number of times I've dumped out every thought and feeling about these books to you, audibly working though possibilities for arcs, resolutions, plot points, and motivations, some of those conversations evolving into utter nonsense (or crossover episodes, like your people crashing Kodi and Aleah's wedding, Aleah and Aheia switching places, the mercs meeting your inner circle out at the club). With *Conduct*, that drive to Estes, wondering if the mercs were strong enough to stand on their own outside of *Mountains*—if anyone would ever care enough to read about them—and you giving me that push to listen to my gut, was pivotal. I'm glad Aleah has Lùc, and I'm glad I have you. Sarah L, I barely knew you when you beta read *Leaves*, and your immediate love and understanding of my characters still makes me all sorts of emo. From the very beginning, you were shipping Kodi and Aleah, and that enthusiasm is part of what spurred me to dig deeper into their story. When I gave you the jumbled, disconnected scenes that I'd cut from *Mountains*, you validated not only that they weren't needed in the duology, but also that these were moments and background that deserved their own limelight. I hope I did them justice for you!

Taylor, the editor in chief of Hardcastle Publishing House (no relation to the throne of comfort): your eyes, both on this novella and the duology, were invaluable. The comments, jokes, and headcanon activities of my characters: priceless. Seriously though, thank you for being a trustworthy opinion and being willing to spend an afternoon doing research to help add realistic elements to certain scenes. *salute* (Also I love that, with us specifically, this could be related to smut or body horror and there's really no inbetween.) I can't wait to make you edit an Achilles tendon moment one day. Lea Ann, thank you for your time and brain power throughout this series as well! I truly appreciate it so much. Apologies for that time you thought I invented the blood eagle, I promise I'm not actually that wild.

Kelsey, Rachel, and Shelby, I know I can only say it so many times before it starts getting old, but I still mean it just as much now as I did with *Leaves*: thank you so much for being with me through this process, for your time, and for all your help! You all (Sarah included) are the *best* team of beta readers. Full stop. I am the luckiest to have you.

To my family, thank you for your unwavering love and support. Josh, you're amazing, and I'm so freaking happy that I get to have you by my side through all of this.

And again, to you, the reader: thank you. To everyone who's ever reached out to let me know how much they enjoyed something I've written: you keep me going. I hope you stick around for the adventures to come. Maybe one day we'll even find ourselves back in Sekha ... but until then, live.

Carissa Hardcastle is a lifelong adventurer and bookworm who will never turn down fast food, still listens to 2000s pop punk, and always greets wildlife that crosses her path. Though fiction has been her passion since she was young, she also spent seven years as an air traffic controller in the Air Force, where she cultivated a love for all things aviation. Carissa grew up exploring the Sierra Nevadas of California, but now lives in Colorado with her husband. Mountains are her happy place, and much of her writing pulls inspiration from the grandeur and magic of the Rockies. When not writing or out finding adventure, she enjoys consuming horror and fantasy in any medium available.